SOIL OF THE GONE

a novella

Valerie Gonzalez Street

VALERIE GONZALEZ STREET

Soil Of The Gone

For Mom, who lived to tell the tale.

To examine the causes of life, we must
first have recourse to death.

- Frankenstein by Mary Shelley,
1818

The Newly Dead

El Guardia was there the day of her funeral. He stood with the girl, who was now one of the dead, towards the back of the cemetery, looking on at the living as they cried and held one another. He expected a cacophony of questions, confusion, and anger from her since that was the rather aggravating custom of the newly dead, but the young girl just stood watching silently. Even in death, a quiet girl who did as she was told, who was quick to learn.

For several years, her family came to the little cemetery every week, adorning her grave with a variety of special treasures because it brought them peace and because they were the things she loved in life. In time, however, it became necessary for them to move further north for work and the visits came less and less frequently. As the years passed, the living who came grew older and more frail. She watched her father's gradual use of a cane, her mother's hands become more and more changed by arthritis. She watched her one living sibling, an older brother, grow and bring a new wife to the cemetery. Then a new baby. Eventually, he became the first to stop coming. And one day, though the girl did not understand how or why, she knew her mother and father would not be returning ever again. Something had gone out, like the light of a candle perhaps. She did not ask *El*

Guardia any questions about it. She just knew not to look for them anymore.

Years of solitude passed for her and she watched her grave and many others around her fall into various states of ruin. It mattered not at all to any of the others, but there was a part of her that longed for the days when she would turn to look upon her tombstone and see fresh flowers or a thoughtful trinket her mother might have brought to leave there. Even so, she worried little about this and mostly looked forward to when she might be received at the gates of a paradise beyond. She needed only to keep herself ready so that when that time came, she could cross over finally, as she believed it had been written. But then they came and brought desecration with them. It was this act of callous cruelty that twisted her then, beyond recognition. Anger engulfed her. It was fueled on only by a singular focus toward vengeance. Yes, restoration would need to be made, but this alone was not enough in her eyes. A price would need to be paid and it was then that she remembered that *El Guardia* was the shepherd they were to entrust with these matters. So she went to him and now she had begun a course of events that no one, not even *El Guardia* himself, could fully anticipate.

"Once this begins, it cannot be undone. We cannot reverse what we will have wrought, child," *El Guardia* said.

There was a time when she was among the living that all of this would have shocked her to her core. That her blind fury would have so shamed her that it would have compelled her to go to her mother weeping for prayer and guidance to rid herself of such destructive inner workings of her mind. But that was then; she was among the dead now. There was nothing left for her to hold on to in any world and no world that wanted her. She had become altered and undone.

Chapter 1 - 1964

Beads of sweat dotted Marta's forehead as she woke up in her bed. She was surging with tension and she sat upright almost immediately. The sound of birds outside her open window and her father giving Mateo instructions on what to load where on the truck out front in the yard helped her get her bearings. It was nearly seven in the morning but the air was already getting thick with the day's heat. Summers could be sweltering in South Texas, so most evenings you left the bedroom windows slightly open to let whatever cool night air existed inside. This helped everyone sleep a little more comfortably.

Marta sat up and moved off the bed, which sat high up off the floor in its old brass, rickety bed frame. She grabbed some jeans and a shirt from her dresser and made her way down the small narrow hallway to the one bathroom in the two bedroom little house, the smell of bacon and *frijoles* coming off the kitchen. She lived in this tight family home with Mamá, Papá, her brother Mateo and her sister Dahlia. Space was limited but they made it work in the little home with Marta's parents in one room, her sister Dahlia with her in the other and Mateo making a bedroom of his own out of the living room every night after lights went out. By morning, he always folded his bedding neatly away off the couch and made the room presentable for family and visitors.

She had been living here ever since her family moved to the town of Harlingen when she was four. Situated in the Rio Grande Valley of Texas in 1964, their slice of Harlingen was dirt roads, street dogs and small houses that stood far apart but were packed with big families. Her parents had worked the fields doing the seasonal rounds of migrant work plus off season jobs they had established for themselves over the years. She had done her fair share of this field work too but once she got old enough to properly protest it, she helped Mamá run the little family store down at the front of the large property instead.

They had to be quick with breakfast this Saturday morning, Marta knew, because today was a cleanup day out at the family cemetery. It was the day every couple of months that everyone, the entire household, went down to the cemetery for a day of mostly yard work. *Las Flores*, it was called. As long as she could remember, she'd been going there with her parents and siblings on weekends. They had never been the professional caretakers of this cemetery by any means but tending to its grounds had become a force of habit for her parents so it had become very natural for the whole family. Now that they were older kids, her parents could rally Marta, her brother and sister to get out there at least five or six times a year. Her parents were there every weekend though, no exceptions.

It wasn't any kind of official family cemetery, although it should have been. Other people not directly related to Marta's family were buried there. But because *Las Flores* was home for many of their relatives gone before them, it had always felt like theirs. It was a relatively small collection of graves on a corner plot of farm land enclosed by a rusty chain-link fence. Over the years, Marta had meticulously studied and learned every grave and tombstone there. All manner of people rested there with some graves dating back as old as 1840, a full five years before Texas became the twenty-eighth state. Some of the dead buried there had lived long lives, some had died young, several unborn even. All of them poor.

Marta always felt a weird kinship with the very young buried there. The children. Nearly all the graves save for the family members Marta's parents tended over seemed largely forgotten. No one had been to visit these tombstones or acknowledge the passage of time for years. Quite a few of the graves of children were among some of the oldest and most neglected ones. The grim reality had always struck her that her childhood, her very youth, was something she had in common with those departed. She felt inexplicably connected to them somehow because of it, and it often felt so real and strong to her that their ghosts seemed almost tangible then.

Still, despite no one in the living world seeming to know or care that these people rested here, Marta grew up feeling that whenever they came to tidy up and look after their own loved ones' graves, they were coming to tend to them all. It was why she used to make a point to stop in front of all the tombstones and to sit an extra length of time with the children. As illogical as it was, her child self at the time couldn't bear this idea that some day we die and then we are left all alone with no one to come care for us.

Now in the bathroom down the little hall, Marta brushed her teeth, splashed some cold water on her face and tied her thick, long brown hair back in a low ponytail. She pulled her jeans on and a loose t-shirt and made her way out to the small kitchen, where Dahlia was already putting her dirty dishes in the sink and washing up her place at the table.

"Slept long enough?" Dahlia cracked before shooting Marta a grin and serving her up some scrambled eggs and bacon.

"You gotta quit reading so late, M. I don't sleep well when you've got the light on till all hours of the night," Dahlia said as she set the plate down in front of Marta, who slumped deep into her seat.

"Sorry," Marta said as she impatiently massaged her temples. She had stacks of books piled up on her side of the room; books of all kinds and reading well into the dead of night had become such a common occurrence that it was enough to set their Mamá worrying for her health.

"Cansada mi corazón cariño," Mamá would often say. *"Aye mijita. ¿Que cosas se te meten en la cabeza?"*

Lately Marta was not merely reading because she always loved a good book. If she was being truthful in those moments where her mother expressed concern, she might have told her that for a few days now, she had been having a very bizarre sort of nightmare that left her feeling frightened and exhausted every time she wrenched herself out of sleep. These dreams always rendered her near immobile in her bed. It was as if her body became too heavy, too weighed down. It took extreme energy and effort to pull herself awake from that wretched sleep every time and maybe it was starting to take its toll.

Now here at the breakfast table with Dahlia, she found herself on the verge of confiding this much to her sister but time was up. It was time to go and their father was hollering for them from the front porch.

"¡Muévanse hijas!" he said. *Move girls!* "We've got to go. The day is getting hot!"

Dahlia went to grab her bag and Marta set her dishes in

the sink before wiping down the table and hitting the kitchen light on her way out. Mamá was already heading down the porch stairs to the truck as Mateo finished loading up the yard equipment that they needed for the long day. Her parents would often have their post breakfast cup of coffee out on the covered front porch in the mornings because they had always been early risers. This was a necessity when you had grown up doing the sort of seasonal migrant work they had known for much of their lives but it also afforded them a chance to enjoy the cooler morning air and quiet solitude that only occurred in those early moments.

Mamá and Papá loaded up in the front while Marta hopped into the bed of the truck next to her sister and brother. This was not an uncommon way for households like theirs to travel if they were headed out for a day of labor like this. They threw blankets and pillows back there some times and in their younger years, it was like a driving slumber party.

"Agárrate para que no te caigas," Papá said before firing up the truck and off they went.

As the little truck moved down the small country roadway, Marta had time to think about last night and a fresh wave of exhaustion swept over her. She had been having the same bizarre dream off and on for days and could make no sense of what it meant. In the evenings, rather than make any effort to get to bed early, she would do whatever she could to put off falling asleep at all. Most of the time she preoccupied herself with a book off the stacks she kept by her side of the bed and started reading. It did not matter that she had read them all multiple times before, she just needed the distraction. A predictable one.

When fatigue would inevitably win out every night and Marta

finally did fall asleep, she would see the same thing in her dream each time. She was always standing in a field out in the middle of nowhere, just barefoot in the dirt. The dawn of morning fog was so thick she could not even make out houses or cars anywhere in the distance, if they were even there. She had no idea where she was. She could never see anything at all that might have given her a sense of bearing. Marta would just stand there rooted in the same place. Waiting for her heart to stop pounding and the fear, like a vice, to release its grip. Marta always stayed frozen and waited for anything that would give her the guts to actually make some kind of move.

The lull of the steady road was all it took. Marta's eyes became heavy and she was not really aware they had begun to close. It might have only been for a moment. When she opened her eyes, she saw the face and immediately recoiled. It was gray, sickly, and its mouth formed a wicked snarl. It looked an awful lot like her sister. Dahlia.

Marta let out a scream, startling Dahlia and Mateo who had both been dozing themselves. She scrambled to a corner of the bed of the truck as they both looked on at her wondering what in the world was happening.

"Good grief, Marta, what's wrong? What??" Dahlia asked.

"*¿Qué pasó?*" their father hollered to them now through the back window.

Marta could feel the truck slowing down as Papá pulled over to the shoulder of the road.

Now fully at a stop, everyone stared at her while she tried to get her bearings. Marta looked around and everything looked right. Dahlia was there, normal. Mateo, also fine. Her parents too. Everybody was clearly panicked and wondering what had just happened but as far as Marta could tell, absolutely nothing had. She closed her eyes, took a deep breath and opened them again. Everything looked as it should.

"Are you okay, *mija*? What happened?" Mamá chimed in.

"I'm sorry," Marta began, sounding dazed, "Yeah, everything is okay, I just thought I saw something for a minute."

Nobody moved, they just kept staring at her.

"I just thought I saw something that startled me but it was nothing though," she said.

It took a few more apologies and meager attempts to explain whatever she had just experienced away enough so that her family bought it, settled back into their positions in the truck and continued on.

It was nothing. Marta kept telling herself that over and over, trying very hard to forget the nothing's hideous face inches from hers.

Chapter 2

The small road out to the cemetery was mostly quiet this time of morning with only the occasional passing car. Marta settled back into her corner of the truck bed and pulled her knees up to her chest. She was completely awake now. Whatever that was, it felt terrifyingly real and Marta placed her hands over her eyes to try to clear her mind of the image of her sister like that. Trying to think of something else, she set her mind wandering back to her first memory of *Las Flores* which had to have been sometime around the age of four or five years old. Her mother had been taking Marta with her since she was a baby. Any time Mamá went out there to do yard work or take flowers or visit on birthdays, anniversaries or special days like *Dia de los Muertos*, she took Marta along. In the beginning, she would just sit in the grass and watch everything around her like any fascinated toddler would do. The visits became far more tiresome for Mamá once Marta was fully mobile though, because she made her way around the little cemetery with alarming efficiency and missed no opportunity to snatch every little thing she saw with her tiny hands, including special mementos right off of graves.

Marta's mother was always quick to correct her whenever that happened because she had taught her children so many things and certainly one of those things was what you do and do not do at a cemetery. You should not, for instance, be loud in a cemetery, if you can help it. There is rarely a need to shout or be boisterous unless by way of mourning. When walking, be mindful that you do not accidentally walk over someone's grave. Observe where the tombstones are and walk around them wherever possible. Be respectful and always err on the side of caution.

"La gente está descansando aquí," Mamá would say. *People are resting here.*

As Marta got older, she would make herself more helpful to Mamá and help pull weeds or pot new flowers to leave on the headstones of their family. She would fetch them water and snacks from the picnic Mamá always packed. She would also lose herself in the cemetery, walking along every single grave to study each marker and headstone. It became a habit, something she made sure to go through and do at least once before they would leave at the end of the day. She also began asking more and more questions as her curiosity bloomed in those years.

"Why does this tombstone have a statue of little shoes on it?" Marta asked on one of their visits.

"That was a baby, *mija*, look at the dates. They may have been stillborn or they may just not have lived very long" Mamá answered, and Marta looked to see that yes, the birth and death dates were either the same or sometimes mere days apart.

There were a few like that as well as a few other graves of children, and Marta made it a point to learn them all. So much so that she felt she had come to know and memorize each of their markers, the dead who rested at *Las Flores*. Though it might have seemed strange, she really loved going there as a child. It made her feel like some kind of keeper of history.

In all her time there, she had always felt the place to be peaceful, except once. When she was ten years old, she arrived with Mamá and Papá for a short work day in the cemetery. Dahlia was home recovering from a cold and Mateo was helping Victor, Papá's right hand man then, run the little store for the morning. Mamá and Papá got to work there amongst the tombstones. Her: pulling weeds and rooting out dead plants that had not survived the most recent frost. Him: mowing and trimming the lowest branches of each tree. Marta was bagging weeds and clippings up in lawn bags, hauling what she could over to the entry gates so they could load them into the back of the truck when they finished for the day.

It was to be such a quick visit; she did not know if she would have time to do her usual walk about to see each grave since there was so much work to get done first. As she filled up another lawn bag and started pulling it toward the gate, a feeling crept over her. Marta felt the sensation of goosebumps forming on her skin. The rise of each individual one. Her heart thumped loudly in her ears and she became very afraid because she was suddenly able to understand exactly what that strange feeling was. It was the unmistakable feeling that someone was watching her. The realization washed over her so fast that she whipped her head around to look all around her, half expecting to see someone hovering behind her. But there was nobody. Her eyes scanned the little cemetery for any signs of anything, but all was as it should be. Her eyes landed on the back fence on the opposite side of the grounds. There was nothing there but Marta could not shake the feeling, the genuine feeling that, despite the fact that all she saw was the grass rustling in the breeze and a vast expanse of nothing but field, something *was* there. Watching. It was the first and only time Marta had ever felt that grip of fear at *Las Flores*. They finished their work, ate quickly, and then loaded up to head home. She did not tell Mamá or Papá about it that day or ever.

As the kids aged out of the years of wanting to be particularly helpful to their parents when it came to things like yard work, they sought out all kinds of excuses to get out of going with them weekly. Even Marta. As she grew up, Mamá had observed with some sadness, how Marta had become something of a homebody. She maintained friendships in the neighborhood, though it was hard for Mamá to know how much of those friendships were truly hers or just Dahlia's friends that she was having the occasional friendly exchange with. After she left high school to be more available for the work up north in the fields, Marta had become quite invaluable to the success of Mamá's storefront in the off seasons. She had begun the shop as a means to make a little extra money, but honestly, Mamá had always had such a good head for business and she truly loved the sense of independence and freedom it gave her. Marta enjoyed the work of it too, doing inventory, stocking the little shelves, even taking on some of the gardening with Mamá, a master teacher, of course. Most of all, Marta loved that it was something that was theirs. They were bound to no one. It was the family business that Mamá had grown from nothing and it was Marta's first taste of what it could feel like to be her own boss. To harvest what they had grown themselves on their own land and feed communities with it. She liked that very much.

Now as a young adult, she rarely walked through *Las Flores* to stop by each and every grave like she did when she was a child, but she still felt she knew them all the same. It continued to be a joy for her to visit, even if she sometimes loathed the manual labor involved. It was kind of like greeting an old friend whenever she went. Neither Dahlia or Mateo ever carried the same sentimental feelings for *Las Flores* that Marta did, however.

"This place is too depressing Marta," Dahlia would always say.

She tended to only focus on the neglect and decay of so many forgotten graves there. For Dahlia, the only good trip there was a short one and Mateo felt the same way. He detested the prevalent thick brush that always tried to take root there; it was a beast to mow down and clear out. Their father often pushed him the hardest, so Mateo had been doing the work of boys twice his age for a long time now. He saw *Las Flores* as merely a nagging problem he dreaded tackling every few months. A problem that would leave them all spent, sore and blistered most of the time. Nothing like the way Marta saw it. She saw it as a place of sanctuary and eternal peace.

Chapter 3

Papá rounded the corner at the end of the road and turned onto Highway 281 where the rows of corn started. They were nearly there. *Las Flores* had for generations existed at the end of this corn field shoved off in the corner much like an afterthought. The owners of the land (and the cemetery), the Mason family, had designated this section of the field to Marta's great, great grandfather, Don Santiago–a man who had worked the fields and served as foreman of the farm for the Masons for most of his adult life. The purpose of this small land offering was so that Don Santiago could bury his family dead and loved ones there. Unfortunately, the patriarch of the Mason family never drew up a formal deed or paperwork laying this out in specific detail, so when he died in 1910, the cemetery fell to his children. They had no interest in honoring the agreement their father had made with Don Santiago, but they allowed his family to bury him there when he died three years later. Despite this land being repossessed by the Mason kin almost immediately after Mr. Mason's passing, they still permitted Don Santiago's family to make use of the burial grounds even after he too died. The relatives who requested it were still being laid to rest there, as well as other members of the community who had known the Mason family or done work on their property at one point or another. By the time Marta was eight years old however, the Mason family had ended the practice entirely, making one of Marta's tíos among the last to be buried there in 1953.

As they pulled up to the rickety gate of the small grounds and Papá turned off the truck, Marta stood up and stretched while she gazed out over the field. The sun was bright all around it but thanks to the mature *cedros* inside the little fenced cemetery, it stood out as the one shaded sullen spot in the entire area. Somehow this too, made it look forgotten and unloved. Without realizing it, and from a young lifetime of having learned it, Marta locked into a pattern she would need to be in for the next few hours: be patient, be deliberate and, most importantly, be listening. Every little noise in the grass, the wind blowing through the cornfields, bugs flying by. But for their movements, Marta and her family were out in the country, all to themselves. The silence was as heavy as the growing heat and it made her listen even harder. Of course, they were not entirely all to themselves out there. The dead were there too. Marta climbed out of the back of the truck with her bag and some of the equipment, ready to work. Despite her peaceful memories tied to the grounds, she had been feeling a sense of unease all morning. It had escalated in the bed of the truck when she had dozed off and experienced that brief nightmare. Now it was intensifying again and she was unable to shake it.

* * *

They had been working swiftly for close to two hours. Mateo was mowing the grass with the little push mower they brought while Papá cleared larger brush that really set off a lot of mosquitos, much to Marta's misery. Mamá and the girls pulled weeds and set about planting new marigolds, positioning fresh flowers in pots everywhere. They were making great use of time and Marta figured they would wrap up the labor relatively quickly. Then they would be able to sit back and relax there in the cemetery with a picnic of bean and potato tacos, water, soda pop and whatever else Mamá was able to round up that morning.

Half an hour later Papá finished giving the grass and all new plants a good watering from the hose. Now he and Mamá were at the faucet cleaning up their hands using the bar of soap they always brought. Mateo, exhausted from how dense the grass had been, sprawled out on the blanket Dahlia had just laid down and she swatted him with a hand towel until he sat up and moved over for the others.

Marta plopped down on the blanket next to him and handed him a cup of water. Mamá always packed two huge thermoses with ice inside to keep it nice and cold. On a day like this, when they had been working like dogs under the hot Texas sun, the icy water cooled their insides better than anything else.

"What time do we want to head back?" Dahlia wanted to know.

Newly seventeen, their Mamá was finally permitting Dahlia to go to the occasional, heavily chaperoned, dance. If she was not heading off to one of those, they could also find her at *El Grande*, the old theater, or a trip to the ice cream bar on F Street in Harlingen where everyone gathered. She'd waged a long, drawn out battle with Mamá over this freedom and their mother only finally relented because when it came right down to it, Dahlia was always far too smart for her own good. Their mother was past the point of having enough energy to keep up the fight. Dahlia was a lovely young woman with the same long brown hair Marta had only Dahlia actually styled hers. She would set it at night with curlers and then whip up some fabulous style with it the next morning. If you ever asked her how she managed to maintain that girlish figure of hers, she would tell you it was all that dancing. She was a fantastic dancer, even Marta had to admit it. Any time Dahlia got out on the dance floor with a beau, all eyes would be on them. She partnered so well she made even the clumsiest of guys look graceful out there with her. All that social butterfly status aside, Dahlia really had her sights on finding someone to settle down and build a family with. She had just started teaching bible school at Our Lady of the Immaculate Heart twice a week. A great looking girl who loves the Lord and children? It was the perfect sort of arrangement for a young woman hoping to appeal to some kind of upstanding young man.

Mateo was a real looker too but if he cared, it never seemed to show. He was the smartest of them all and he would definitely become the first of them to make it as far as college if he kept saving as well as he did. He was more than amiable with everyone and highly skilled. There was probably no shortage of young girls in the community just waiting for him to look their way but Mateo always seemed to have his eye out for a one-way "anywhere but here" ticket. Getting saddled with anyone in Harlingen was the last thing he would ever dream of.

As for Marta, at this point in her life, there was not much of a plan. Marta was older than Dahlia by two years, but had no actual sense of urgency to embark on the next chapter of her life. She helped Mamá run the family store and tracked inventory. She also helped tend to the gardens that provided their produce and helped maintain the house. Marta loved to read about adventures and places to travel to, but mapping out such a life for herself was another thing entirely and one she struggled to put any kind of focus on.

Still, her mother would have liked her to have some sense of where she would like to find herself eventually in life. She wondered if Marta's contentment had become complacency and whether Marta would come to regret that, eventually. The simple reality was that Marta could not envision a life that took her too far from her parents. Whether they would admit it or not, as they grew older year after year they relied heavily on all their children to do their part caring for the house and the family business in ways neither Mamá nor Papá could quite manage on their own anymore.

"I suppose we've done enough here," said Papá, who was setting up two lawn chairs for him and Mamá. "We can leave after we eat," he added.

Mamá passed around pre-made sandwiches and the rest of the picnic she had packed way too early that morning. The food was always especially delicious whenever the workday had been as grueling as this. They devoured the packed offerings and then stayed under the shade of the old *cedros*, talking about Papá's next work trip up to Ohio in September. The plan was to visit some relatives there and to commit to a scheduled field job he had lined up on a farm. Mateo would go along on this trip to help in the fields and Marta and Dahlia would help Mamá run the shop selling *raspas*, tamales, *pan dulce*, plus the fruit and vegetables she grew herself in the garden.

As Marta started packing up trash with the rest of the family and rounding things up to take back to the truck, she noticed Mamá walk over to one of the larger, older trees surrounded by a few tombstones. Marta noticed her Mamá was carrying two buckets she had pulled from the truck earlier when they first arrived.

"What are you doing? Do you need help?" Marta called to Mamá as she walked over to join her.

"There's a lot of good soil here," her mother answered, motioning to the dirt. She handed Marta one of the buckets. "Let's collect some in these and we'll take it back with us."

She had good cause to think so anyway. Mamá knew that many of the graves here were quite old and because these had all been poor farm workers or nearby residents in the rural community, it was highly likely they had been placed in the cheapest wood caskets available at the time, probably little more than a box. The people here buried their own; there would be little use of more modern embalming techniques. That could mean the soil had little of the potential for mineral contamination that more modern caskets and materials could impart. Knowing none of this, however, Marta flashed her mother a look of repulsed confusion.

"You want to take *this* dirt? What makes the soil so great? The dead people buried in it??" Marta quipped, in spite of herself.

"Marta, por Dios! No seas asquerosa!" Mamá said, exasperated with her oldest daughter.

Marta wanted to argue the point that what her mother seemed keen to do was what was actually gross here, but she decided against it.

"Look," Mamá said, gesturing to the ground before them, "nobody's buried here. I wouldn't ask you to take soil from an actual grave, Marta."

Marta chuckled, her first real moment of levity all morning. It felt good to be playful with her mother and share a laugh. She helped shovel up dirt quickly and dumped it into the two buckets Mamá had set out for her until both were full to the top. Then she called Mateo over to haul them both back to the truck as they all quietly walked away together.

Chapter 4

She was standing in the field, barefoot in the dirt, and the fog was too thick to see through, but she knew she had been here before. At that moment, the fog began to clear and Marta could see *Las Flores* there just a few feet ahead. She had no idea how she got here, knowing it was too far for her to sleepwalk there somehow.

While she stood there groggy, the sudden realization that someone was watching her came over and in that moment she began to make out a dark shadow at the farthest fence line of the cemetery from where she stood. She could not really make out too many of the shadow's features, but she believed it to be a person; it had the shape of one at any rate. The figure stood hunched over a good deal, with its arms hanging low at its sides. Marta thought to call out to it, to say something at least, but something inside her got the better of her and she could not make a sound. The hairs on the back of her neck stood on end. The more she looked at the shadow, the less it looked like a human at all. Fear started to seize Marta. Her breathing grew short and quick. She wanted to turn and run, but she could not take one step. She did not dare to break her focus as she kept her eyes on this figure just standing there.

And then, before she could process what she was looking at,

the figure pulled up to its arresting full height and launched itself forward, racing toward her at a speed faster than Marta's eyes could even understand. It bared glistening teeth and Marta could clearly see the hideous, pointed fangs snarling at her. It was not human at all and all Marta could do was stand there frozen. She opened her mouth to scream but no sound came out.

* * *

Marta woke up in a panic and scanned the room for any signs of intrusion. She was terrified as she looked around, half expecting to find someone there besides her sister. Just like in her dream, she could not move. Her fear had such a chokehold on Marta that she just sat there in her bed. She pressed herself into the corner of the wall, staring out at the quiet room, trying to calm her heart down. It had felt so real, her dream. That thing, that figure running toward her felt as real to her as her sister asleep over in her bed. Marta clearly had not been screaming out loud in her sleep at least and for that she was relieved because that would have woken everyone and sent the entire house in a panic.

She did not get a good look at what it was, even despite how rapidly it was coming for her. Its shadowy features never came into better focus for Marta, just those wretched fangs growling at her. She closed her eyes and could clearly see it back in that field, preparing to run at her again. That debilitating fear had not gone away now that she had come back into the waking world. Marta looked out the window, afraid of what she might see, but thankfully all that was there was the lawn dimly lit by a half moon. Everything in its place.

* * *

A few hours later it was properly Sunday morning and Marta rolled over in her bed to stare at the ceiling. She had finally drifted back to sleep after that nightmare, but she kept slipping right back into variations of the same bizarre dream. At one point, she dreamed she was back in the cemetery with her mother and she was a little girl again, running around the graveyard, playing in her own make-believe world with the growing sense that she was being closely watched. As soon as she felt a presence drawing closer to her, she would wake herself up. In another dream, she was balled up asleep on the ground in the yard and the same dark shadow was there, standing at her feet. Just as it began to move up closer toward her face, Marta pulled herself awake, shaking with fear. She did not understand why exactly but it was that seemingly simple act, the act of waking herself up each time, which somehow took maximum effort for Marta. Like trying to run as fast as you can in a dream and getting nowhere. It was the damnedest thing; as exhausting as it was futile. Now that it was time to get up this morning, she felt utterly worn out. Drained of all her energy.

When Marta stepped out into the living room, she saw Mamá through the window out in the front yard pruning in the garden. The truck was gone, which meant Papá and Mateo were off picking up lumber to start the shed expansion build out back that Papá had been plotting for a few weeks now. He wanted more space to store tools obviously, but also a covered space he could work in when he had furniture repairs to do. As a means to bring in steady work in the off seasons, he had begun a woodworking and handyman business that year and showed a natural skill for the craft. Everyone in the community called upon his services, and it was something he was truly proud of. He had even made some beautiful furniture pieces from scratch that were his own design. Marta's parents were easily the hardest working, most adaptable people she knew and truth be told, she felt pretty *perezosa* by comparison.

The rest of the house was pretty quiet and she scanned the small living room and kitchen, wondering where Dahlia might have gone off to this morning. Maybe she had walked over to visit her friend Yoli (Yolanda) who lived a few blocks away. Marta had no friends in the neighborhood to speak of. Even though Yoli was fun to be around and always welcomed Marta whenever she would join her and Dahlia out at *El Grande*, Marta definitely considered her to be more Dahlia's friend and herself merely the tagalong or, more frequently, the chaperone. Then Marta remembered it was not yet eleven so the church would not have let out yet, which meant Yoli would not be home. Dahlia, Mateo and Marta had worked out a deal after a lot of relentless badgering that on weekends when they went out to labor with their parents at *Las Flores*, they could all forgo church services the next day so everyone could rest up and recover for the following week. In truth, as Mamá and Papá got older, they too very much appreciated this deal because it let them also get the rest they needed for their various aches and pains.

Marta made her way over to the cupboard and pulled down a glass, which she filled with water at the sink. Just as she brought the glass up to take a sip, her eyes glanced out the sink window to the backyard and there was Dahlia. Her back to Marta, standing stock-still. Something about the rigid way Dahlia stood there was awkward, though Marta was not immediately sure why. Just a feeling, she supposed. Marta set her glass down and opened up the back door to go check on her sister.

"What are you doing out here, Dali? What are you looking at?" she asked.

Marta was trying to catch her breath as she made her way out to reach her sister in the middle of the yard. Whatever the house lacked in size the lot it sat in more than made up for. To be standing smack dab in the middle of the backyard was to be a fairly long distance from the back porch. Mamá devoted the far right side of the back to several rows of planted vegetables that produced beautiful harvests every year. On the other side of their back fence was open land that led out to the Arroyo Colorado, an old distributary of the Rio Grande. The kids had years' worth of memories playing back there during the day. It was not a safe place to go wandering in at night though, and Mamá and Papá kept the fear alive with old ghost stories about a woman out there looking for her children who might take them if they wandered too far toward the water. *La Llorona.*

"Did you hear me? What are you doing?" Marta said again as she got a little closer.

It was when she turned to face her sister that Marta immediately cried out and jumped back, horrified. Dahlia's face was ashen. There were just hollow, dark sockets where her eyes should have been. She seemed to be in some kind of trance. Before Marta could fully assess her sister's condition, Dahlia's neck jerked sickeningly to one side and her angry, ghastly face locked onto Marta's. Marta screamed out and Dahlia shoved her hard, sending her several feet across the yard. Marta hit the ground in a painful heap, but she immediately scrambled to her feet to run. In that moment, Dahlia dropped down to the ground, her body snapping and twisting in inhuman ways. She began running after Marta on all four limbs. Her body had morphed into what now looked like a wild animal. Marta let out a blood-curdling scream and turned to run, already painfully aware that she had no hope of getting away.

She tore open her eyes, screaming, as she pulled herself up to the head of her bed. Marta was in her room, but it took her several minutes to realize it. Mamá came running in and saw Marta, her body balled up with her face buried in her hands.

"*¿Qué te pasa?*" she asked. Marta was visibly overcome in a way her mother had never seen from her daughter, and it scared her. "What is it, *mijita*? What's wrong?"

But Marta did not have an answer. Her mother held her and tried to give comfort, but even after a few minutes, she still could not find words to describe what had just occurred.

"You had a bad dream?" Mamá offered.

"Yeah," was all Marta could answer, and she felt a chill like cold fingertips creep down her spine then.

* * *

When Marta finally emerged from her room a little while later, the house was quiet. The day was overcast, but that did little to bring down the late morning heat. She looked out the front window and could see Mamá had returned to the garden work that engrossed her when she heard Marta screaming and ran inside. No one else was around as far as Marta could tell. She went into the kitchen and reached for a glass up in the cupboard. She could not help it. Her eyes glanced out the sink window out of habit and she went cold. Because there was Dahlia. Her back to Marta, standing stock-still and rigid. Marta's heart was pounding in her chest. She turned back to look at her mother, still in the garden out front, and then flipped her head back around to stare out at Dahlia. Seconds ticked by that felt like too many minutes and Marta, petrified, could not think straight. She inched over to the back door and went to grab the doorknob, hesitating for a moment. Her breath coming in loud exhales, her body shaking uncontrollably. She opened the door just enough and tried calling out to her sister, but Dahlia did not move. Marta scanned her surroundings to get her bearings. The sky, the heat, the dry breeze that made it feel like a convection oven out there in the yard. *It feels so real*, she thought. But it did in her dream too, and fear gripped at her again as she made her way out to the porch. Marta decided she was safest to stay there on the porch and she called out to her sister again, louder.

"Dahlia?? What are you doing?"

Dahlia jumped and jerked her head around, startled. Marta's whole body relaxed and she immediately let out a sigh of relief.

"What?! Jesus, Marta!" Dahlia wore her irritation on her face so well at times that all she had to do was toss Marta a glare and it would make her wince.

"Sorry. But what are you doing out here? What were you looking at?" Marta asked, making her way down the porch steps.

"I was just… out here," Dahlia said, mumbling as her face softened.

"Are you okay?" Marta asked, looking at her sister more closely now. The morning's events had left Marta feeling raw, but she could see that even Dahlia looked out of sorts. Dahlia turned to look at her and immediately tried to relax her posture a little before clearing her throat.

"I don't know. I just had a really weird dream last night and then couldn't get back to sleep. There were these noises that I kept hearing and it just– I don't know. I just got spooked," she said, finally pulling her thoughts together to form something that sounded like maybe it could be coherent.

"You had a nightmare?" Marta asked, instantly feeling less alone. "Me too, I kept having these terrible dreams all night. What was your dream?"

"I was standing out here, like I am now. And there was somebody standing at the back gate there," Dahlia said, gesturing to the chain-link fence across at the end of the backyard.

"I couldn't see who it was and I remember thinking maybe it was Mateo or something, but this person… seemed larger. Everything was too dark. It just looked like a shadow to me from here. It scared the shit out of me and before I could do anything, it started… running toward me and I screamed hard, Marta, but that's when I woke up," Dahlia told her.

She had her arms folded over her stomach, trying to present herself as collected and nonchalant, but Marta could see the goosebumps on Dahlia's arms.

"I didn't go back to bed after that. It was already light out at that point, so I just got up and started making the coffee. Mamá and Papá were blown away that one of us would be awake," Dahlia said. At this, she smirked and relaxed a little more.

Thankfully, Dahlia did not focus too much on Marta in that moment as she turned to head back to the house. She was chattering on about needing to get going because she had hoped to visit Yoli later for lunch. Dahlia did not notice that Marta was not immediately behind her. She was standing still in the yard where Dahlia had left her. Immobile. Marta stood there, unable to make any sense of the reality that her sister had somehow, on the exact same night, been plagued by nearly the same nightmare.

Chapter 5

She had been a dragging around all morning. Marta was going about her work so bone tired and in need of a nap, but there was too much to get done to prepare for the week ahead. She had jarred up some of the pickled cucumbers that they would have on the store shelves in a few weeks and was about to start doing a stock check of the abundant tomato harvest they had already had this season. She felt so drowsy she thought she might collapse. It was half past ten in the morning now and the sun was so punishingly bright outside that the birds corralled at the little bird bath on the side of the house in the last holdout of tree shade they would have before it shifted with the morning light.

She set her apron down on the counter for a moment and shuffled over to the couch in the living room, where she plopped down immediately. *Just a minute*, she thought to herself. She would just rest for a minute and try to recharge for a bit before finishing up with the tomatoes. But it was that brief pause in motion that proved all Marta's body needed and she closed her eyes, drifting into the sleeping world soon after.

Suddenly Marta was staring down at her bare feet, moving in wild motion through the tall, wild grass in the half dark. She realized she was running and yet the speed at which she was going made it seem more like leaping over vast patches of ground, traveling at a speed she knew she just could not go in reality. She looked up to see where she was but could only get so far as seeing that there were feet running out in front of her too at a similar pace. Whoever she was with, they were both racing through this field together. Whether that was from something or toward it, she could not immediately tell.

Marta turned around, trying to see if anyone was behind her, but she could only make out a cluster of small shadows getting more and more faint as it became clear she was racing away from it. She recognized the field then and the little fenced in cemetery with its tombstones being the little shadows, she realized.

Just as she was about to whip her head back around and race forward to catch up to the other set of legs, she caught something out of the corner of her eye. One of the low shadows in the cemetery. It seemed taller than the others, but that was not what she noticed. What caught her eye was that just in that moment, with unbelievable speed, the shadow rose up and moved right for the gate.

* * *

Marta flashed her eyes open and sat upright on the couch, gasping in huge breaths of air. It was still daylight. She looked at the clock and saw that she had not been asleep that long at all. Maybe twenty minutes. She adjusted her body to move her feet to the floor and sat there, still trying to slow her breathing and steady herself. Every time she pulled herself out of one of these dreams, it was like when she and Mateo were just little kids swimming in the canal out behind their house. They would swim as far down toward the bottom as they could and then the race was on as they scrambled to the top. More than once, Marta remembered pushing it just a little too far. Holding out in the depths just a little too long, so that she was fighting to reach the surface before her lungs gave out. That was what waking up from these wild dreams felt like. Like she was fighting to get to the surface where she could open her eyes and gasp for air. As her body released some of its tension there on the couch, she felt more exhausted than she had been before she ever sat down.

Who was with me? Marta thought about the other pair of bare feet. Her dream had not revealed the full picture for her. She had no idea who she had been running with, or why it seemed like they were running near the cemetery, but a cold chill went down her spine again when she pictured it. Marta felt the distinct feeling of weightlessness in the dream. They were leaping across the field as fast as they could in the pre-dawn light, desperate to put distance between themselves and *Las Flores*, but why? Marta got up and started moving back to the kitchen. Her mind still felt groggy but her body was on high alert. She made quick work of tallying and carting up the remainder of the vegetables before stepping outside for some fresh air.

Out on the front porch, it comforted her to see that she was not alone. Papá and Mateo had made it back at some point and they were tooling around with the truck engine. It was old and it required what seemed like almost daily tweaks and repairs. Some days, it really just felt more like Papá had a love of fiddling with cars and Mateo was more than willing to jump in and assist. They took no notice of Marta as they busied themselves and chatted, so she sat down on a porch chair in the shade, staring out at the yard, trying to relax for a minute. These strange dreams she had been having were taking on a very different feel now. Before, she had mostly been experiencing them with a sense of eerie bewilderment, but now she was struggling to know what was even real. She had to rip herself awake every time, and it left her shaking with fear afterward. To add to her growing misery, she still had no idea what was bringing them on. Now it seemed like Dahlia had experienced something very similar in her sleep at least once as well. She would need to go to Mamá with it, Marta decided. Mamá would break out her rosary or, knowing her, lead her in some kind of cleansing. A *limpia*. Religious rituals or superstitions maybe, but these soothing forms of prayer were so much a part of their family, their life story really since they were born, that these simple acts their mother engaged in were always enough to calm Marta's fears growing up. Maybe then she could finally get a decent night's sleep.

All day long she had been on edge. Marta's body had become hardwired to react to every sound she heard, every movement she thought she detected. She could not tell if she was just being paranoid or if she was intuiting correctly that something was off. When Mateo had come in later that afternoon, letting the screen door slam behind him while Marta had been just off of the kitchen in the washroom, she startled so badly that she scattered laundry soap all over the floor. Her nerves were so frayed by this point, she knew it was lack of rest as much as it was her growing fear to even let herself fall asleep in the first place. There was a heaviness in the air she could not shake. It was this inexplicable feeling of something watching her. Weighing down on her. It was almost as if it were hovering overhead, eyeing her intently as she moved about the house.

"*¿Qué pasó?*" Mateo called out from the living room when he heard the soap cup drop and Marta cursing to herself.

"Nothing," she answered, muttering. "You scared me half to death is all."

"Are you okay?" he asked.

As Mateo rounded the corner to see how bad a mess Marta had on her hands, he found her crouched down on the floor looking dejected with dark circles under her eyes that drew emphasis to her narrow face, making her look downright gaunt.

"You look awful. Are you sick?" he asked.

"Thanks," Marta answered, shooting him an irritated look. "I'm tired. Slept terribly last night. So did Dali. She said she had a bad dream."

Marta filled him in on very general details about some of her nightmares and on Dahlia's dream as well. She did not say anything about her dream of Dahlia out in the backyard, hideous and deadly. She emptied the broom pan into the kitchen trash can and set the broom back against the wall.

"Sounds pretty messed up," Mateo said.

"What about you? How'd you sleep last night?" Marta asked, turning to her brother, realizing she had not had a moment to check in with him at all yet.

Mateo shifted his eyes away from hers and seemed to glance out the back window before turning around and walking over to the living room, where he slumped into the recliner.

"Fine," he said as he propped up his feet. His face registered the slightest bit of strain that nobody but Marta could have possibly picked up on.

Such a bad liar, Marta thought.

"What do you mean? Did you dream about something? You dreamed something, didn't you?" Marta asked as she moved over to the living room, eyeing her brother carefully.

He was the lone son of the family, but as he had now grown into a young man, he towered over all of them, so much so that his size seemed even more comical when paired with any of the dainty furniture in their house. It was like living with a giant sometimes. As it was, his feet hung off the side of the couch every night when he made up his bed on it. All the same, he was the baby of the family and Marta could be just as concerned and protective over him as if he was still a little boy at times. It annoyed the living hell out of him. He was never one to really talk excessively with anyone about his thoughts or emotional life, but then he also did not have to because he wore those emotions as plainly on his face as if they were the clothes on his back. He had no poker face, never had. Marta always knew when her little brother was holding out on her and she knew all she needed to gain information from him was patience. He continued to avoid meeting Marta's stare for a minute, but then he finally looked up at her and stilled his foot from twitching.

"I was running in this field. In my dream. I don't know where I was, but I was barefoot and just *sprinting* in this field, Marta. Faster than I've ever run in my whole life," he said, momentarily impressed with his own athletic ability, even if it was the product of his imagination while he slept.

Marta said nothing but stared silently at Mateo with growing panic in her body. She had not told Mateo about the dream on the couch, and Dahlia had been out for much of the morning after that moment in the backyard so he would not have heard it from her either.

"I don't know why, but I was chasing somebody and I was terrified out of my mind. It felt like I was gonna die, swear to God." he said.

* * *

That evening at the small little dinner table in the kitchen, the family lost themselves in their normal conversations but Marta could feel something in the air that made her wary. Looking around the room at everyone, she could see the fatigue on all of their faces. She wondered if maybe Mamá and Papá had also been having rough nights of sleep lately.

As they all wrapped up dinner, Mateo excused himself outside to lock up some equipment before it got too dark. Dahlia and Marta cleared the table while Mamá sat there and pulled out some of her sewing. Meanwhile Papá moved into the living room to watch some of his shows. When they were little, Mamá had made all of their clothes by hand. She was an excellent seamstress, and even now she made many of the party dresses that the girls wore for dances or for church events. She had taught her daughters how to sew as well and together they had grown up making clothes for all their dolls before taking on projects like pillowcases, curtains, pants, blouses and, in Marta's case, book bags.

"I'm going to bed early and you better not wake me up with your late night reading Marta," Dahlia said wearily.

She gave her sister a tired but still playful side-eye before making her way over to the couch to watch television with Papá. Marta grinned after her and then rinsed off the last of the plates before turning back to Mamá, whose eyes were deeply focused on her stitching.

"Mamá, I need to tell you something," Marta said as she drained the soapy water from the sink.

"Ok," Mamá answered. Her eyes briefly flickered up to her daughter's face and then went right back to her handwork,

"What is it *mija?*" she asked.

Marta dried her hands and sat down at the table, racking her brain for where to even begin. She was looking at the dirt under her nails, trying to find her words, when her heart stopped cold at the sound of it. A low, monstrous growl. Marta immediately noticed the goosebumps on her arms as she came to the horrifying realization that it was emanating from her mother's direction.

She looked up to see Mamá's face transformed. The rows of pointed teeth bared, the sharpest of fangs catching Marta's attention immediately. Eyes so dark and large, they looked like two black holes in her hideous face. No light shone in them, it was like staring into some dark abyss. Marta screamed and pushed back up out of the chair, slamming into the little hutch that held extra dishes, nearly sending everything clattering to the floor. She flung herself around and threw open the back door, racing down the back porch only to be stopped at the sight of Dahlia. She was standing out in the middle of the backyard, almost exactly as she had been earlier that day. Except this time, Dahlia was facing Marta. Staring right at her with that same face the color of ash. Waiting.

"Marta!" her mother's voice snapped so loud inside her brain that Marta jumped in her own skin.

Her head was swirling so dizzily that she nearly fell over, but her hands gripped onto the sink hard, keeping her upright.

"Marta, oh my God! Are you okay??" Mamá jumped up from the table and brought her hands out to catch her. "What's the matter??"

Hearing the commotion, Papá sat up a little more upright to peek into the kitchen. Marta still had her hands gripping the sink, her knuckles white. She kept her eyes on the soapy water that was, in fact, not drained at all. She winced ever so slightly when she felt Mamá's hand on her shoulder. She slowly turned to face her mother, and it was only once she saw Mamá's face, as it should be, that Marta exhaled.

"I'm sorry, I–" Marta began before taking another breath to collect herself. "I just… um. I don't know what happened."

She looked around the little kitchen and over at the little hutch that just moments ago, she had nearly knocked over. Turning her eyes over to the back door, she could see that it was still closed. She could even see Mateo out there by the shed, as he said he would be. Everything in its place.

"You were going to tell me something and then you just went silent. What's the matter? Are you feeling sick??" Mamá asked.

Her face was full of worry, and she gently pulled Marta over to have a seat at the table.

"Yeah, I'm sorry," Marta said again, "I just… I thought I saw something, I guess."

"No," Mamá said, and it was the way she said it that made Marta's eyes meet her face again. "That's not it. There's something wrong, and you are going to tell me. What is it?" she asked.

"Dali and Mateo and I… we've all been having these terrible dreams. Together, over and over. I don't know how to explain it," Marta said, and she realized she *did not* know how to explain it.

The fear she had been experiencing in these nightmares was so real and so vivid. She could make a safe bet judging by Dahlia and Mateo's faces when they spoke about their own dreams that it was no less terrifying and disturbing for them too. But now, as she sat aside from her mother, Marta was already regretting bringing it up because she felt there was no way she could fully articulate what was happening. What had just happened. Truth be told, she was starting to feel a little insane from it all as she stared down at the checkered tablecloth. She was about to say *nevermind* but out of the corner of her eye, she saw Mamá's hands reach out as if to touch her. She looked up and saw Mamá staring back at her closely with her brows furrowed. The fear was unmistakable. Whatever Marta's face was silently conveying, Mamá could see it plainly. It was then that Marta realized she had been sitting with her hands in her lap and that her body was visibly trembling. She wanted to cry.

"What is it?" Mamá repeated gravely.

Chapter 6

Dahlia and Papá were watching TV together. *Bonanza* was one of Papa's favorite shows, and the pair sat in the dim light of the living room enjoying the program together. It provided some much needed normalcy to the atmosphere of the house, which had otherwise been very heavy for Marta since confessing her dreams to Mamá that evening. Mamá had grown up learning traditional prayer and healing methods. She may not have been as much the master in that particular realm as others in her family were, but there was no denying her green thumb and her devotion to their faith or prayer. She immediately set her mind to worrying about why these nightmares had become so chronic so quickly for Marta.

"You're under too much stress, aren't you? You need to take a break from the store," she said, but Marta quickly waved this off.

"No, Mamá. I'm not stressed out. What I am is tired," Marta answered, somewhat impatiently.

"Then that's what it is. You are exhausted, Marta. This is what happens. When our souls are weary, we are always at our most vulnerable. We're at our most susceptible to attack and that's when dark imaginings can enter our mind and evil fears start attaching themselves to us like shadows. Because we've unknowingly opened ourselves up for that attack," Mamá said.

And then, as an afterthought, she added, "Or it's the damn books you're reading."

"So that's it? It's either stress, fatigue, or my books?" Marta shot back, and she realized she would not be smarting off to her mother so much if she was not so physically and emotionally wiped out.

If Mamá heard the nasty tone though, she ignored it. She got up and went over to her little altar set up in her room to light candles and begin reciting the Rosary for her family. She left Marta to finish tidying up in the kitchen alone. After Marta did that, she went out to the back porch to check on Mateo, since he had not come back inside yet.

"I'm almost done," he said as he glanced up to see Marta emerge on the porch with house lights illuminating her head from behind.

"You need any help?" Marta asked as she watched her brother haul their father's massive tool box to the shed.

"Nope. This is the last of it," he hollered over his shoulder as he placed the box in the shed and put the padlock on the door to close it.

"I told Mamá. About your nightmare. And mine. All of ours, actually," she said as Mateo made his way up the steps to join her on the porch.

"*¿Porque la preocupas Marta?*" he said, throwing up his hands in immediate frustration. "You think that was really necessary? It's one dumb dream. It means nothing."

Mateo plopped down in the dirty old folding chair next to her and stared hard out at the back fence, sulking. He was angry he had told something in confidence to his big sister and she had gone and squealed.

"It hasn't been that. Not for me," Marta said, trying to get Mateo to meet her eyes so he could see she was not fooling around.

He was distracted fishing around his pocket for his lighter, having put a fresh cigarette in his mouth. Their parents hated that he smoked, but they knew they could not chastise him too much. Half the men in the rural community had adopted the smelly habit at significantly younger ages than Mateo. Even more so among the harvesters in the fields. And to be fair, Mateo at least smoked pretty sparingly, resorting to it only when he was particularly stressed or otherwise unhappy.

"I've been having nightmares every night for almost a week now and it's been getting so much worse. I can't...I can't tell when I'm dreaming anymore," Marta started. It embarrassed her to say it but it was the truth.

"I'm afraid to close my eyes, Mateo. I swear I'm starting to see things even when I'm awake. And then for you and Dali to have them too and they all sound so similar? Of course I told Mamá."

She was aware that as she told this to her brother, her voice was cracking a bit. It felt like she was unraveling. Marta did not know what would be in the dream world waiting for her and worse, she was beginning to wonder what would happen if she could not wake herself up to get away from it. Mateo heard her voice shift. He put the still unlit cigarette away and gave her his full attention.

"What do you mean you *can't tell when you're dreaming*? You said you had a bad dream last night, you didn't say you've been having them all week. You should have said something sooner. What's going on with you?" he asked.

"Don't know, but Mamá's help, whatever that might be, can't

hurt at all, Mateo. I can't keep going like this. I haven't had a normal night's sleep in so long, I feel like I'm going crazy," she said.

Marta's voice sounded almost hoarse now. He could fully hear the stress and sleeplessness in it. She had been battling something on her own, afraid and tormented by night terrors she barely had language to describe. There were countless worries and pockets of sorrow that Marta had always carried on her own about the life she had hoped to have and the life that was. Not just for herself, but for all of them.

The poverty they had known all their young lives coupled with the generations of degradation and general racism that come with growing up brown in the south had a way of stomping ambition out until it was just dust and sediment in the earth's soil. Very few people had made it out of the neighborhood to better things and that was no coincidence. Who was to say what Marta might be doing at this point in her life if some of these realities had simply been different. Mateo wondered then at the slight leg up he had over his older sister when it came to what their futures held for them. He was Mamá and Papá's only son and he had always grown up with the full understanding that he could do no wrong in their eyes. He had every God-given gift necessary to be successful at life, not the least of which was the basic fact that he was a man. As he looked at her quietly, he realized Marta had been on her own battling something these last few days when she had clearly needed someone. Some kind of comfort. Silence fell between them then for a few minutes and Mateo's gaze drifted downward before landing back out at the back fence. The dying light of day faded as the early stars of the night presented themselves for the two siblings to behold.

"*Lo siento,*" he said without looking at her because there was not much more that could be said. "I'll stay up tonight, ok? You won't be alone."

At that, Marta let herself rest her back against her chair then, feeling just a little bit of relief.

* * *

Mamá had long since finished her prayers and gone to bed. She was no night owl like the rest of them. Marta could see as she came back in through the back door that Dali had fallen asleep out on the couch and Papá's eyes were slowly closing as the light of the TV illuminated their faces. While Mateo washed up in the bathroom, Marta stirred Papá to move on to his bedroom with Mamá for the night as Dali silently stumbled off, still half asleep, to the girls' bedroom.

Mateo settled onto the couch, now his bed, and finished off the rest of the *Ed Sullivan Show* while Marta sat up in the recliner with the lamplight on and the public library's copy of *The Bell Jar* in her hands. Outside, the wind was picking up a bit and that brought a most welcome breeze through the partially open windows in the living room, causing the white curtains that Mamá had made to sway gently back and forth. Everything about her surroundings was so peaceful in that moment, so relaxing, and before long her eyelids grew heavy and the words on the page became fuzzy. She closed her eyes and slipped into sleep.

It was dark outside, but Marta could see that everything in her room was in its place thanks to the faint light of the moon through the window. She lay in bed and tried to resettle herself under the covers, but she stopped short when a faint tapping started in from above. Her whole body alerted to the sound and she listened hard. The taps were small but unmistakable. They seemed to be moving closer to her room. The more Marta strained to hear, the more she got the distinct impression that these were actually footsteps she was listening to.

Someone is on our roof, she thought, and immediately wondered if anyone else in the house was hearing this as well.

She looked over at Dali, but she was sound asleep, undisturbed. Just as Marta turned to look away from her sister and back to the ceiling for more footsteps, she saw it in the doorway. A faceless dark shadow that looked to be the size of a person. It began moving quietly into the room, expanding its reach across the walls and corners, inching its way closer to Marta's bed. It petrified her in that moment to realize she could not scream. Her voice could do nothing. She also realized she could not move. Inside, her mind was frantically panicking. Marta tried to wrest her limbs into any kind of movement off the bed, but she was frozen. Rooted in terror lying there. *This is evil,* she thought. Marta remembered what her mother had said about dark imaginings.

Evil fears start attaching themselves to us like shadows.

Suddenly Marta knew she was dreaming. This had to be another night terror. The shadow was nearly at her bedside now. Marta tried again to move her body but it was no use. In her desperation, she started reciting the prayers Mamá had taught her. She convinced herself that the power of those words could drive this evil away and it was almost strong enough of a belief to calm her heart. Before she knew what was happening, the shadow lurched forward and grabbed Marta's arm. It was ice cold, like nothing Marta had ever felt. It made her gasp out in pain. She could now see that the shadow was not faceless at all. Two black eyes locked with hers and its frozen grip tightened around her arm, so cold it burned. Before she could open her mouth to scream, the evil thing sneered in her face.

"Tus palabras no te ayudarán ahora," it said. *Your words won't help you now.*

Marta tore her eyes open and gasped in air as she startled in the recliner and scanned around her. The living room was quiet and her reading light was glowing warm yellow overhead. The television had switched over to the "Star-Spangled Banner" for the night and Mateo was softly snoring on the couch. She listened with her whole body but could hear nothing else in the house. Marta sat there a moment and tried to get control of herself. She kept running her eyes over every corner of the room like a caged animal. Her breath was still coming out in ragged gasps and her eyes darted over every entrance, exit, doorway, and window. The windows were still open.

Violently shaking, she got up and closed every window in the living room, sealing them with the latch. She moved over to the kitchen to close the window above the sink that overlooked the backyard and she looked out the window just as she had done earlier that day. The wind had been gently swaying the trees but suddenly everything stopped. Mamá's curtains became perfectly still. Unnervingly still. It was as if she had slipped into a vacuum somewhere. All the natural sounds of the outside had stopped as well. The summer crickets, the wind chimes that Mamá put up around the corner of the house toward the front yard. Marta stood frozen to the floor as she looked out the window and saw an unmistakable shadow hovering at the back fence. And just like in the dreams that had been torturing her mind for days, she could not scream.

Chapter 7

The moon cast its milky light over so much of the yard but not where the shadow stood under cover of the *mora* shrub, which had grown so lush and tall that the kids had always considered it more of a blackberry tree than a bush, back when they were younger. For a split second, Marta considered that maybe this was another dream. She frantically looked back over the living room to where she had been in the chair and half expected to see herself still asleep, just having some weird out-of-body experience. No, this was real. Marta whipped her head back around to the window, horrified to see the shadow was now standing *in* the backyard, on her side of the fence. It could no longer be called a shadow anymore at this point because it was now bathed in moonlight and Marta could plainly see every ghastly detail.

The creature stood hunched with its head tilted at a sickening angle to the side. Right away, Marta could see it was not human, or at least not wholly human. It stood on its hind legs and its form very much resembled that of a gray wolf. Its black eyes looked right at her as it let out a low, sinister growl, baring all of its hideous pointed teeth. Marta stopped cold. She took in the deadly claws on each arm and even the ears seemed to be pointed like a wolf's. Marta stood motionless and terrified at the sight of this creature straight out of hell and again she wondered how this could be real. This had to be a hallucination brought on by not enough sleep. Up to this point, the creature, for all its wretchedness, seemed to move so slowly that Marta could have assumed it was injured or frail even. No sooner did she take a small step back though, the thing raised up to its full form. Marta could see its impressive height and broad shoulders, briefly giving the appearance of something more human, but only for a moment. It quickly dropped down so that all four legs touched ground and it lunged forward in an unnatural sprint, faster than any animal she had ever seen. Marta's eyes could barely comprehend it. Within seconds it leapt on to their porch and growled so loudly Marta covered her ears. She let out a blood-curdling scream and instinctively threw herself back in the opposite direction to bolt. She nearly crashed full speed into Mateo in the living room. He had leapt off the couch in a sheer panic at the sound of her screaming.

"What is it?! What is it??!" he shouted. He was on his feet, holding her by both arms, his eyes wild. Dahlia, Mamá and Papá were now all in the room, frantically looking around confused.

"Something is outside!! It's trying to come in!" Marta said, not recognizing the sound of her own voice. It sounded so raw. Her eyes darted all around the room, looking for any kind of weapon.

"Whoa, hang on. Marta, hang on," Mateo said, trying to calm his own voice. "What happened?"

"It's outside. It's right outside! It's going to come in!" she screamed and her eyes checked every window to see if the terrible beast was now there.

A break in, Mateo thought, and he ran to the back door and flipped on the floodlight on the porch so he could scan the full yard. Seeing nothing, he opened the back door and stepped outside, Papá now joining him.

"*Mateo, vuelve a la casa,*" Mamá hissed in a whisper but nobody listened.

Marta held her breath and grabbed a kitchen knife off the counter.

"*¿Quién es? ¿Qué viste?*" Papá called out, demanding to know information, trying to hide the panic in his own voice now.

As far as Mateo could tell, everything looked undisturbed. He grabbed the flashlight off the porch rail and darted off toward the shed to make sure nobody was hiding out in there while their father hollered something about grabbing a shovel. Outside, Mateo could see that the lock on the shed was secure. He turned and saw Papá's flashlight now moving about the perimeter of the house, shouting at whoever could hear.

"*Será mejor que te vayas de aquí!*" Papá said. *You better get out of here!*

The house and grounds looked all clear. There was no one else out there. Mateo's breathing and muscles relaxed a little as he made his way over to Papá. Together, they went back up into the house. Inside, Mamá had turned on the lights so she and Dahlia could quickly search through the full house just for peace of mind. Marta sat on the couch staring at the ground. When Mateo and her father entered through the kitchen, she could see the look on her brother's face. She knew what he was going to say already. His expression was pensive as he tried to figure out how he was going to reassure her everything was fine, that she was just confused. She buried her face in her hands and let the tears run down her face, her body still shaking. She felt like she was going insane. It was now one in the morning and she had wreaked havoc on the entire household with her hysterical imaginings.

"We didn't find anybody," Papá said to the room as he locked up the back door and set his shovel against the wall. "Whoever it was, they're gone now. I'm sure we scared them off."

"You're staying up too late, Marta. *Estas agotada,*" Mamá said. *You're exhausted.* She was showing her own exhaustion as she placed a hand on Marta's head.

Marta looked up at her then, incredulous. It was just earlier that evening that her mother had validated her fears that not only was this real, it could be something not of this world. Something trying to grasp at Marta's spirit. That she was vulnerable. Now Mamá was dismissing these experiences as little more than the troubled hallucinations of a sleep deprived daughter. But then Marta remembered her father was present and Papá simply never entertained these kinds of beliefs. He felt they were more folktale or lore designed to scare children. Mamá would never talk about these matters in front of him.

"We all need to go to sleep. Let's go, lights out," Papá said.

That closed the matter for the moment, and Papá took Mamá's hand as they headed back to bed. Marta stared after them sadly. She turned then to look at Mateo and Dahlia, expecting them to be doing the same thing, only to find their faces fixed on her. They had both been watching her intently the entire time.

"What did you see?" Dahlia asked.

* * *

Marta shared every horrid detail, leaving out nothing. The image of the creature burned into her brain and every time she closed her eyes, she could see it right outside the backyard window and she was terrified all over again.

"That's twisted. You were dreaming, Marta," Dahlia said when Marta finished. The three of them were all sitting at the kitchen table speaking in hushed whispers to try not to disturb their parents.

"That's just one of the nightmares," Dahlia added, sounding convinced.

"No Dali, I am not making this up. I swear to you this was real. I don't know what it was. It was this… beast," Marta said, trying to hold up her hands, desperately trying to convey the size of it.

Even as she said this, she could not even fully believe it herself. Marta knew it all sounded ludicrous. How could this possibly be real? This had to be her mind playing tricks on her. A deranged, sleep deprived mind trick.

Mateo had yet to speak, but he had been trying to listen to them both while also straining his ears to listen for the trespasser should he, or *it*, decide to come back. The immediate concern he had was in keeping the house secure. He was not sure what to make of his sister's story. He did not believe in this stuff anymore than his father did, but there was no mistaking Marta's terror. *That* was undoubtedly real. Something out there had scared the shit out of her and he knew the only way he could help was to either show her everything was safe and there was never any danger to begin with, or that whatever or whoever it was, he could drive them away.

"Look, I'm going to just take the flashlight out one more time and walk around the house. After that, I think we should maybe all try to lie down, ok? We've stayed up long enough and whatever it was, it hasn't come back," Mateo said quietly before standing up and heading out the back door once again.

Marta could not conceal how irritated she was. She knew what she sounded like, but for as much as everyone thought her head was perpetually in the clouds, she never made up wild stories. She knew what she saw. Even so, she could not argue with Mateo's sense. It was true; the creature had not come back. There had not been so much as a peep outside and they had been awake for a couple of hours now. The best they could do was maybe try to get some rest and make better sense of things in the morning. That was a rational enough thought anyway, but a gut-wrenching fear kept Marta far from even considering the possibility of sleep.

"Come on. Let's try to go to sleep and we will figure this out tomorrow," Dahlia said, as if hearing her sister's thoughts, and she stood up to motion Marta to join her.

Marta reluctantly got up and made her way down the hall to the bathroom to splash some water on her face and get ready for bed finally. Just as Dahlia was moving around the small house turning off lamp lights, Mateo walked back in and gave her an *All clear* look before locking up the back door one more time and setting his flashlight on the counter. Dahlia gave him a nod of agreement like she already knew this information and waved him goodnight as he collapsed on his bed on the couch. She eagerly sank into her own bed, ready for the chance to fall asleep at last, the sound of the bathroom sink running as her sister washed up her face. Everything would be alright in the morning. Marta would see. Mamá was right. This is what happens to an exhausted mind that has been having nightmares for days. On this point, Dahlia could relate because it was not like she had been sleeping so well either. That dream she had the night before was, to put it mildly, unnerving. It felt so real for her as well. That was when Dahlia recognized what she should have caught hours before, when her sister had been sitting dazed on the couch and her father was running around the outside of the house trying to scare off what he imagined were just some dumb kids. The dream Dahlia had of someone standing at the back fence, someone hunched and in the shadows. This was exactly what Marta said she saw while she was awake.

It was right then that Dahlia heard it. The sound was faint but distinct. It was competing with the sound of the bathroom sink still going while Marta washed up, but Dahlia could still hear it. Light taps over in the corner of their room that seemed to be coming from the ceiling. Just a few and then nothing. Dahlia could not be sure, but she thought it sounded very much like footsteps.

Chapter 8

She took after Papá in that she, too, had a more pragmatic approach to most things. Dahlia did not really lose herself in books like Marta often did. She did not disappear into the world of study like Mateo and she did not lean too heavily on things like religion the way Mamá would whenever hard times came about. Sure, she taught bible school, which pleased her mother to no end, but as far as Dahlia was concerned, this was a paying job, not a calling. It was simple work. She liked the kids and that was enough for her. She always tried to keep her focus on the things that were within the realm of her understanding and ability. This had a way of allowing her to streamline life in a way she preferred; in a way that was comfortable and familiar to her.

This was why Dahlia chose not to say anything the next morning about what she thought she heard from the ceiling while Marta had been in the bathroom. She decided it could not have possibly been the footsteps it sounded like, because Mateo would have seen someone on the roof when he had done his final walkabout before turning in for bed. Also, Marta had clearly barely slept, so she did not need this extra information, which would only set her on edge even more. She had fits of night terrors for much of the night based on how many times

Dahlia heard her stir. She tried to stay awake a little while so that Marta could peacefully drift off, knowing someone was keeping vigil nearby and it seemed to work for a little while at least. Not long after Marta settled in and said a weary goodnight to her sister, her body could no longer fight the exhaustion and she fell into something of a fitful sleep. Part of the other reason Dahlia had committed to staying up for a bit was also to listen for anything else that sounded like footsteps or something on the roof. Thankfully, it remained quiet and almost peaceful. Eventually fatigue took hold of her too and she slipped into a heavy sleep as well, waking periodically to the sounds of Marta gasping for breath.

Marta had very little respite in the night. She could not tell what was real now. The world around and her world within, their edges were bleeding into one another and she felt her fingers slipping on their grasp for what was left of her mind. It's a terrifying thing, she thought to herself as she climbed into bed. To not know your own mind anymore. Or more specifically, to come to the sickening realization that you can no longer trust it.

The creature was in her dreams, monstrous. A gigantic wolf-like creature standing in the yard. It was still staring at her with those vacant black eyes, growling, fangs bared. No matter how much she wanted to turn and run, it was like its eyes locked her in place, immobile. Just as she had been at the window, she felt frozen in fear in her own dreams. She could neither scream nor move and only with what felt like every ounce of strength she possibly had was she sometimes able to wake herself up. Swim to the surface.

At another point in the night, her dreams found her back in her bedroom. The dark shadows at the door seemed to be moving to post up in the four corners of the space and they all turned on her, laying helplessly in her bed as if they were setting up for an attack. When she did finally wake up later that morning, in the full light of day, she instantly felt shame and embarrassment. The memory of confiding in her brother and sister only to realize they simply did not believe her then came rushing into her groggy thoughts and suddenly she was wide awake and angry.

Marta got dressed and made her way out to the living room, where everything was quiet. She knew her mother and father were outside at the little shop because she could see them through the window, conversing with the neighbors and customers about the lush produce they had this morning. Dahlia was probably at the shops, picking up a few more groceries to bring home before heading out to the church to work. The only one who had finished high school was Mateo, and that was only because he had argued with Papá about it relentlessly until he finally got his way. Papá fully expected him to join the regular rotation of work with the rest of the *braceros.* The ones who labored in the fields. Instead, he found a way around it to go on to actually graduate from high school. He was now working to save up enough for some semesters of college. Dahlia had left school after her sophomore year and Marta had made it only as far as halfway through junior year. It was an incredibly difficult thing to keep up with studies and the picking seasons in Texas, Ohio and Florida, places their family traveled to every year for work. Dahlia taught bible school on Wednesday evenings and Sunday mornings, but the rest of the week she worked in the church office as the front secretary. She loved it because her co-workers were nice and they entrusted her with a number of tasks, but her favorite thing about the job might have been the rule that office attire was required. Dahlia was always eager for any excuse to dress it up. She would draw out an idea of what she liked and then find the material to pull the outfit together. Mamá had sewn her many a new dress, blouse and skirt just for these days where she got to dress up and be inside a different life for a while.

Marta saw the plate of food with a napkin over it on the kitchen table and she knew it was intended for her. It was a breakfast of potatoes and eggs with fresh tortillas. She sat down starving and began to eat. The tortillas were still warm, the potatoes cooked to crispy fried perfection, and Mamá's homemade *salsita* in a bowl nearby. After the night of terror plaguing her mind while she pitifully tried to sleep, she could now taste the comfort and love in her Mamá's food and it was enough to bring hot tears to her eyes while she ate quietly. She had been withstanding days upon days of an all out assault on every one of her senses and it left her feeling so weak and small sitting there at the kitchen table. It made her feel broken.

Once she rinsed off her dishes and wiped down the table, she stepped out to the front porch and took in the day. Marta was pleasantly surprised to find that though the sun was beaming brightly across everything, there was a nice breeze in the air keeping the scorching temperatures at bay for the moment.

"Ahí está ella! ¿Como dormiste mija?" Papá said, greeting Marta and giving her a loving hug as he joined her on the front porch and motioned towards Mamá out at the little storefront.

"I slept fine," she lied.

"I didn't hear anything else the rest of the night. Your mother didn't either. I think whoever it was you saw, they were probably just kids cutting through our yard, or maybe it was Ignacio trying to make it home," Papá said, letting out a laugh.

It was true that now and then, one of the men in the rural community, Ignacio, could be seen stumbling down the road, drunk as a fish. He was one of the sweetest, quietest men Marta knew, but when he had a few drinks in him, he would always end up ambling down the dirt path, belting out *corridos* as he made his way home. By the sheer grace of God always, he got home safe to a wife who lovingly put him to bed so he could wake up with an angry headache the next morning.

"I'm certain it was coming for the house," Marta said wearily, thankful her father didn't seem to catch the word *it* that she had accidentally let slip.

"I'm just going to go help Mamá. Let's just forget about it," she added, attempting to feign shrugging it off.

If trying to discuss it with her brother and sister last night was a taste of just how much understanding she could expect from the whole family, then it would be fruitless to discuss it any further with Papá. As far as he was concerned, *maybe* she saw an intruder, but they had long taken off by the time he and Mateo had gone out to investigate and that was that. She caught her father's approving nod, a sign he was ready to put this behind them, and flashed her a quick smile before heading inside. Marta waved him off and as she did, her focus shifted over to a dark line just inside on the windowsill. It stood out amongst the creamy white paint of the house and her first thought was that they now had ants to deal with. She popped back inside to more closely examine the trail and quickly realized it was not ants at all. Instead, a long, fine line of dirt was there along the sill. The line was razor sharp, perfectly aligned dirt and Marta blinked to make sure her vision was straight and that it was not in fact ants. She silently lamented how tired she must be that her eyes were playing tricks on her and brushed the dirt into the trash before heading back out toward the shop.

Mamá was bagging up tomatoes for Señora Garza, who lived further up the road. She had known Mamá since they were in grammar school together, though the two had never been particularly close then. Señora Garza's family had a little more means growing up than Mamá's family, and she always found subtle ways to make sure Mamá never forgot that. Time is always the great leveler, however, and in the winter that Señora Garza turned thirty-two, her husband of sixteen years died of a blood cancer, leaving her to use what savings they had to try to hang onto their home and the land. She had been struggling to make ends meet for years and Mamá had become a great friend to her in that time, always reaching out to see if she needed anything and sending Mateo over once every two to three weeks to mow around the property or take care of any home maintenance Señora Garza might have. She was nowhere near as enterprising as Mamá was and she had come to greatly admire her friend and all the hard work she put into her successful shop, seeing her for the self-made woman Mamá was.

"Gracias corazón," Señora Garza said to Mamá before waving to Marta as she got into her little old car. *"Hola Marta! ¡Te ves bien mijita!"*

"Buenos días, Señora Garza," Marta said, waving back, and she mustered as good a smile as she could. She certainly did not *feel* great, but it was good to know she at least looked presentable enough to the outside world so as not to cause concern.

Mamá offered her no such delusions, however, when she said, "You look tired Marta."

"I am," Marta answered back.

"Your father says he didn't hear anyone else the rest of the night, so that's good. Probably just kids cutting through the yard," Mamá said, echoing her husband. Hearing this yet again made something in Marta snap and she raised her voice to her mother louder and more firm than she would have intended.

"What I saw wasn't a child, Mamá. This wasn't human," Marta said. Mamá stared at Marta hard, immediately understanding her daughter was not exaggerating but merely trying to communicate. She also recognized that the reason must be that Marta had seen something far more horrible than she had let on the night before.

"*¿Qué estas diciendo, Marta?*" she said as she quickly glanced around to make sure nobody was approaching the shop while they talked. "You better start talking to me right now."

Marta sighed heavily and launched into her recounting one more time, hopeful that maybe Mamá would be a more receptive audience than Dahlia and Mateo. She told her about the dream in the living room early in the night when the shadow gripped her arm, the icy cold feeling that felt all too real and the way the shadow sounded when it said her words would not help her now. She described the creature in the yard and the way it stood there; this monster of a creature running towards her with fangs bared wide, ready to attack. She described the horror of being unable to move or make a sound as the creature raced toward the house. Coming *for* her. Mamá stood there with an expression that finally seemed to match what Marta was feeling on the inside. She wrapped her arms around Marta and whispered words of prayer to God before taking her daughter's face in her hands, looking her in the eyes.

"We need to bless and cleanse the house. *And* you. Whatever this is that's plaguing you, we need to purge it from our home, Marta," Mamá said. Marta understood the necessity for this and was ready for whatever her mother was proposing because there was one thing she knew for certain now: She could not take another night of this. She was rapidly losing her grip and there was little recourse left for her.

Your words won't help you now.

Once the early afternoon's heat picked up, Marta and Mamá began boxing up produce to close up shop. As Marta followed her mother into the house, she glanced over at another one of the house windows and noticed another trail of dirt. Again, a razor sharp fine line, unnerving both for its exactness and the fact that this was Mamá's house. You simply did not find dirt like this in her home *ever*; she kept it immaculate. Marta looked at it more closely and scanned back across the porch to the first window she had seen with a similar line. She then walked into every room and checked every single window on every side of the house. Every single one had the exact same thing. A thin fine line of dirt so precise and deliberately placed that Marta could only stand there bewildered. An ice cold fear crept up the back of her neck when she considered for the first time that there may have been someone else in the house with them last night.

Chapter 9

Guadalupe Balli Fuentes, Tía Lupe to Marta and the family, was Mamá's older sister. Marta's Mamá always saw her as a natural healer, growing up in their family home. Someone they might have called a *curandera*, once upon a time. She was frequently called upon to treat and pray over everyone's ailments, both the physical and the spiritual. As Mamá's elder by six years, she schooled Mamá well in all her methods; ones that were passed down to her by Ama María, Marta's great grandmother. Mamá and Tía Lupe grew up devout in the Catholic faith, something they both still carried into adulthood. Tía Lupe had even wanted to become a sister with a convent so she could walk what she thought to be her called path at one point in time. Instead, she met and fell in love with Tio Francisco when she was eighteen and they were together for the next twenty-two years until his tragic passing in a road accident. She never fully recovered from that heartache, and she had been alone ever since.

Now at fifty-eight years old, Tía Lupe still towered over most people she came across, and she carried herself with a quiet strength that Marta had always been in awe of when she was little. She had raven hair with patches of silver showing through and she usually kept it pulled into a severe low bun that pulled focus to her high cheekbones and beautiful, dark eyes. Those eyes held the memory lines of years of smiles and joy. It was impossible not to sit up and take notice of her. She commanded your attention, sure, but she also commanded your sincerity. There was never any rushed conversation with Tía Lupe; she would not let you get away with one-word answers in a conversation or any hastily ill-thought opinions. She strode up quietly to the porch steps and greeted Mamá, who had been waiting for her at the door.

"Hola amor. ¿Cómo estás?" Tía Lupe asked. She hugged Mamá gently as she was ushered into the house.

For a while it was just the two of them lost in conversation on the couch, Marta little more than a fly on the wall and Papá thankfully gone to a new worksite in town where teams of workers were crafting a new house in a developing community. Had he been present, he might have grown suspicious of what they were conspiring about. They spoke quietly, relaying the latest family news and going over the details of what had happened in recent days. It was all so calm that it was a direct contrast to the turmoil swirling within Marta as she sat quietly watching the two sisters in awe. After a good deal of catching up and planning, they were ready and it was time to get to the grim matter at hand. Tía Lupe directed Mamá to go through the house and open up any windows that were closed. She then stood up and went to Mamá's altar in the bedroom, where they both lit candles and recited a prayer together. After that she headed into the kitchen where she began burning *palo santo* and sage to perform *la limpia*, moving about the house, working methodically. This would both cleanse the house and restore balance. She brushed the sage over every door, every corner, all the beds, the furniture in the living room, and then she moved to the first of the windows.

"*¿Qué es esto?*" she said, looking uneasy at the fine line of dirt on the windowsill.

Marta had shown the dirt lines at all the windows to Mamá and she had been very disturbed going through the house examining all of them. She instructed Marta to leave them as they were so Tía Lupe could look them over.

"It's on every window. I don't know how it got here, but it wasn't there when we all went to bed last night," Marta answered.

Tía Lupe quickly went to every window in the house to see for herself the uniformity of every dirt line, how each one was laid out with a perfect peak in the middle going down the full length of it. She started sweeping the smoke of the sage slowly over one of the lines, and the women watched in quiet horror as it disappeared before their eyes. Mamá gasped. Marta rooted herself to the ground, unable to move or speak, her eyes transfixed on the windowsill where the dirt had been a mere moment before. She could not believe what she had just seen, but Marta continued to watch as Tía Lupe went over to the next window and, with a slow sweep of smoke above it, made the line of dirt disappear there as well.

"This is what they used to call the soil of the gone, *mija*" Tía Lupe said, a pained look on her face. "There are spirits not at rest in your house," she looked to Mamá and Marta, her tone low, "Something is here that will not easily leave."

* * *

After Tía Lupe cleansed the rest of the house and followed up with the *palo santo,* she rid Marta of any possible *mal de ojo* for good measure and then it was time to go. She lingered on the porch, hugging Mamá tightly as if they were about to endure a long absence from each other.

"Estoy orando por ti, mi corazón," she said, and she made the sign of the cross one more time over Marta's forehead before hugging her and whispering one more prayer over her niece.

I am praying for you, my heart.

Then she was gone. The house had felt safer than it had in days while Tía Lupe had been there those few hours. Marta could feel her fortifying the house and the people in it, and she felt a wash of relief come over her. Now that she was gone, Marta felt uneasy all over again. The very walls that had enclosed and comforted her for the majority of her life now felt sinister, and nothing in the house was to be trusted.

Dinner was, for Marta, a quiet affair and rather than risk doing or saying anything that would give Papá suspicion that something was wrong, Marta and Mamá let him do most of the talking with Dahlia and Mateo chiming in. Marta had not yet told them about the dirt.

Soil of the gone, her Tía had called it. She meant the dead.

Mateo and Dahlia only knew that Tía Lupe had paid the house a visit and that seemed to be enough to put them both at ease that she made everything right again. Marta wished she could say the same, but she had been on edge all evening. The sky was getting darker and she wondered if the creature would return. She could barely think about it. It sent her mind into such a violent panic. After dinner, Mamá and Papá sat outside on the front porch to enjoy the last light of day and the early evening breeze. They sometimes sat out there for hours, talking and reminiscing. The kids loved it when they were little because as long as their parents were out there, sometimes talking into the late night hours, it meant the kids could run around playing in the yard well into the night. Some of Marta's happiest memories were those nights running in the grass after her brother and sister, the sounds of laughter and conversation from the adults in the background.

Marta and Dahlia did the dishes while Mateo sat at the table with a book and, for a moment, Marta thought about how to proceed. She figured they would think the windowsill dirt as fantastical and imagined as the wolf creature in the yard, but she was counting on the fact that this time she had Mamá and Tía Lupe to vouch for her. They saw it too. This wasn't something Marta saw in a panicked, half-asleep state.

"Tía Lupe performed *una limpia* this afternoon," she said.

Neither Dahlia nor Mateo registered any kind of reaction. These practices were so commonplace for their family and their Tía. It was not extraordinary in the least; it was just the occasional necessity. Like a good spring cleaning, sometimes a house, even a soul, needs *una limpia*.

"Something here spooked her and Mamá and I don't know what to make of it," Marta continued on, making sure to rope Mamá into this part of the story as well, setting herself up for the best chance of success at convincing her siblings this was all real.

Dahlia wiped her hands clean and rejoined Mateo at the table as Marta moved to sit down with them. She told them about the eerily perfect lines of dirt along the inside of all the windowsills in the house, how they seemed to appear overnight. She told them that when Tía Lupe tried to cleanse them, the dirt vanished before their very eyes, that it was evidence to Tía Lupe that something was here that could not leave. *Soil of the gone.*

"I've never heard of that," Dahlia said, her face skeptical.

Mateo leaned back in his seat and tried to process what his sister was saying. This was inconceivable to him, but he knew that Tía Lupe had a lifetime of experience with matters of the spiritual world. He did not pretend to know what his Tía was talking about, nor had he ever tried to. When it came to these kinds of things, Mateo always kept his head down and focused on his work. That had been his way.

"Has Mamá ever heard of it?" he asked, suddenly remembering the next best vessel of knowledge to Tía Lupe was his own mother.

"She had no idea," Marta said, "But I guess she assumes it means we're being haunted or something."

Mamá absolutely believed in ghosts, and on some level, Marta guessed she always had too. Maybe it was the way that she felt connected to the people at the family cemetery. She felt drawn to those souls and considered them as much a part of the living world as if they were truly still within it. *Was that not a form of believing in ghosts?* She had always assumed her brother and sister believed these things on some level, too. After all, there was plenty of gathering around campfires and sharing of ghost stories when they were kids and they had all been raised to hold reverence for the dead. Looking at their faces now, however, Marta realized that this might all be a bridge too far for Mateo and Dahlia. She could see them working hard to make sense of what they were being told and once again, Marta felt terribly alone. Worse yet, night had fully fallen and she had no idea at all of what to expect.

Chapter 10

Mamá and Papá had come in from the porch and were getting ready to retire to their room for the night. Even though the evening was still relatively young, even by their standards, Papá had to be up early and on a new job site in the morning, and Mamá wanted some time to work in her garden before opening up the shop. This was best done before the morning heat settled in.

"We're going to all stay up tonight, ok? We'll stick together and just watch out for anything that happens," Mateo had said and Marta and Dahlia both agreed.

Marta shuddered at the mere thought of seeing the creature again. The image of it was still cemented in her mind. Every time she closed her eyes, she saw it there in the yard and the same fear that rendered her powerlessly immovable gripped her all over again. Dahlia and Mateo finally seemed at least a little more receptive to the idea that there was considerably more going on in the house than they initially thought. With the television turned down low and Mateo quietly reading in his chair while the two sisters attempted to distract themselves with *I Love Lucy* reruns, the house settled into a peaceful quiet that evening. Marta allowed herself to release just the slightest bit of tension in her shoulders. She was not alone after all, and that endowed her with a particular level of resolve that she felt she had been missing as of late.

An hour passed when they all heard it. Marta heard it first and softly elbowed Dahlia next to her. Their eyes both traveled up to the ceiling. Mateo was already on his feet, turning the volume down on the television. It was light at first, the softest footsteps one could imagine, but it was consistent and as the steps crossed the length of the house toward the back door, they grew considerably louder. Faster. Someone had to be on the roof this time. Mateo charged towards the back door, loudly throwing it open, flicking on the porch and floodlights of the house.

"¡¿Quién está ahí?!" he called out and Marta took note that her brother had run out there armed with nothing to defend himself with.

She raced to join him, grabbing his old baseball bat from the washroom on the way out. Mateo flew down the back steps to get further into the yard so he could see the roof. The flood lights illuminated the yard several feet deep and he shielded his eyes to look over them so he could scan what was overhead. He thought he could barely make out a shadow of someone and he shouted at the figure again before racing around to the side of the house, trying to get a better angle. Marta moved to run with him before he redirected her.

"Go around the other side, check if you see anyone!" he shouted, then he was gone.

Fueled by adrenaline that overpowered her fear, at least for the moment, Marta did as she was told. Clutching the bat, she raced around the other side of the house, which was much darker since it did not have the advantage of the angle of the flood lights that illuminated the yard mostly in the direction of the shed. She was reminded of this once she reached the far side of the house and her fear returned. Marta stood frozen in her spot, but she looked up, scanning the roof as Mateo had done. She thought she could hear him shouting on the other side, but she could not hear exactly what he was saying. Then all those sounds went away entirely and a blood cold terror overtook her as she took in the sight above.

There *was* someone on the roof. A young woman, probably not much younger than Dahlia, hovered there, staring right back at Marta. Her eyes were jet black, and it was only after a few seconds that Marta realized that what she was looking at was just black holes where eyes should have been. The young girl's hair was dark like Marta's and long, braided with the tail of it resting over her shoulder. Her skin was the color of ash. Even though it was definitely footsteps they had all heard earlier, Marta could now see that this whisper of a girl floated in the air in a long white gown. There were no feet that Marta could make out. Her expression seemed vacant, but Marta could feel such an intense anger and sorrow emanating from the girl that it stole Marta's breath away.

Who are you? What do you want? The girl seemed to know Marta's thoughts because an answer to her questions popped into Marta's own mind almost immediately:

Yo he venido por ti.

The girl had answered her. *I've come for you.*

It was Mateo's shouting that snapped Marta's mind back into focus. She screamed his name as she raced around the corner to the front of the house.

* * *

Mateo was experiencing something else entirely. He rounded the opposite side with his eyes on the roof the entire time, shouting for whoever was up there to get down. Instead, the figure he thought he saw seemed to vanish before him. What he did see at the front of the house, crouched down underneath the *fresno* tree was something utterly inhuman that stopped him cold. A huge beast hunched there, growling at Mateo and he froze, realizing he had nothing to protect himself with. It had the shape of a wolf, except as it stood up on its hind legs to its full height, Mateo realized it was at least partially human. The thing before him now was some kind of hideous man with grotesquely sharp fangs and claws. Its movements seemed feeble at first, but when it emerged out of the shadow of the tree, Mateo could see its entire form and understood its full physical power and strength. This was the monster Marta had told Dahlia and him about. The creature they did not believe was real. Mateo could only stand there and look on, his mouth gaping. Afraid to take a single step. It said nothing to him, but the creature eyed Mateo closely, its black eyes boring into him so that Mateo could not look away. He took a step back and the wolf matched it with a step forward. Just then he heard Marta shout out for him and that was when he turned and sprinted toward her as fast as he could, praying he could somehow outrun this beast if it followed.

They nearly slammed into each other, running at full speed. When Marta caught sight of Mateo's face, his eyes wide with a fear she had never seen in him before, she grabbed his hand and they ran back toward the back porch, up the stairs. Back in the house, they slammed the door shut and locked it, then slid the small kitchen hutch over to block the door. Dahlia watched them in a wild panic as Mateo ran to the front door and checked that it was still locked and secure.

"*¿Qué está pasando?*" Papá asked, coming out into the living room just then, squinting his eyes at the harsh kitchen light.

"What's going on, Mateo? Why are you guys out there shouting? What's happened?" Mama asked. She was right behind Papá, echoing his words.

"Who did you see?" Dahlia asked Marta, but Marta said nothing and kept her eyes on the back door, listening for any sound.

Mateo killed the living room lamp light by pulling the plug out of its socket and then peered out the front window through the curtains. The creature was either gone or it had moved around to the side of the house somewhere, out of view.

"Mateo, what's going on?" Papá asked again, his voice firm this time, demanding an answer. "Is someone out there?"

"It's the thing Marta saw last night," Mateo finally answered. Hearing this, Marta's head snapped around to look at her brother for herself.

"What? You saw it?? Where?" she asked.

"It was out in the front. It's real," he said, and he made eye contact with Dahlia as he did so.

"What are you talking about, *mijito*? WHO is out there??" Papá asked, reaching for his shoes now as he motioned for Marta to hand him the bat.

Before Mateo could respond, all the lights in the house cut out, leaving them all standing around in the dark with only the light of the moon coming through the windows. The window fan in their parents' bedroom stopped and all the house stood in a silence so heavy that Marta held her breath.

"Marta," Mamá said quietly. She turned to her daughter and their faces silently exchanged all the answers that needed to be said. The house was under attack.

"Dumb kids!" Papá muttered. "They're out there tripping the circuit breaker. Let's go, Mateo, grab a flashlight."

Mateo did not move at first, but their father was already flipping on the camping lantern they kept in the little hall closet, and then he unlocked the front door. Mateo looked around the living room hurriedly for anything he could use as a weapon but came up empty. He ran to the kitchen and grabbed the sharpest cutting knife they had. Then he crossed the length of the house in three steps to join Papá, who was already out on the front porch.

"Close the door behind me and keep watch at the window, Dahlia," Mateo said before leaving. Fear had rendered Dahlia immobile but hearing this, she sprang into action, shutting the door and immediately peering out the window.

"You saw it too?" Mamá asked, but Marta shook her head.

"I saw a girl on the roof. She was… it was a ghost, I think. She told me she's here for me," Marta said. The hairs on her arm prickled as her mind re-lived that moment out around the dark side of the house.

Dahlia stood there at the window and looked back and forth from her sister to Mamá. She could not keep up with her thoughts. Her heart was racing. She was worried about Papá and Mateo out there. Mateo had seen the same creature Marta had seen, and now Marta was saying she saw someone on the roof. That meant the noises Dahlia heard on the roof last night when they were going to bed *had* been footsteps. This was all a living, waking nightmare.

"*Dios mío,*" Mamá whispered.

She pulled Marta over with Dahlia to hold them both, and Dahlia looked out the window again for any signs of their father and brother.

Chapter 11

Mateo was trying to hold the flashlight steady for his father while his eyes darted all over the place, the roof, the front yard, the back. He held the knife close and was ready to lunge at anything that came their way. Papá had insisted they check on the shed first to make sure no one had broken in to hide out or make off with any of his equipment. The lock on the shed door was undisturbed, so they walked their way over to the breaker box by the side of the house. Mateo thought he saw a figure move in the shadows far off toward the back of the yard, beyond the reach of the floodlights, but he could not be sure.

"We need to hurry Papá," he said, cautioning his father. Papá moved quickly, flipping the switches. Lights came on in the bedroom windows and Papá closed the box loudly, causing Mateo to jump.

"Let's go," said Papá.

They took a few steps toward the front and this time, they both heard the steps run up close behind them. There was no mistaking them. They were the footsteps of something loud and large rushing them from the back. They sounded so close that Mateo and Papá both swung around, prepared to face an attack. Mateo hollered out. They stood there breathing hard with their flashlight pointed at the darkness of the yard, but there was nothing there. Mateo looked all around them frantically, but everything was quiet. Whatever they had heard was not there now.

"Let's go," Papa said again. They hurried back to the front porch.

The minute they stepped back inside, to the relief of all the women in the room, footsteps ran the length of the roof from the back to the front of the house. Papá heard the steps and he ran back out to the porch, shouting for whoever it was to come down.

"*¡Baja de ahí, tonto!*" Papá shouted.

Marta moved quickly then. If the beast was still out there, Papá would be no match for it. If the young girl she had seen before was out there, maybe Marta could figure out what she wanted and get an answer to all of this. A way to make it stop. She ran out to the front steps to look over the roof. There she was, the young girl, hovering there with the same hollow eye sockets, black, vacant. She seemed to be watching Marta all the same. Marta looked to her father to see if he was seeing the girl also, but it did not appear that he could. Instead, he took off around the corner towards the back, continuing to shout at nothing.

"Come down from there, fool!" Marta heard him yelling.

Mateo followed behind him. Papá had no idea what else lurked out there, and none of them had any real idea how dangerous it could be.

"Get back in here, Marta!" Mamá said, shouting out of the front doorway. Dahlia was staring out the window wide-eyed at her sister, terrified.

At that moment, the girl on the roof turned as if to walk away except she vanished right before Marta's eyes and that was when Mamá cried out, hearing the footsteps on the roof running towards the back of the house this time. The lights in the house cut out again. Dahlia and Mamá shouted again for Marta. She could see their frantic faces through the window. Without thinking, she ran around the corner toward the back to look for Mateo and Papá. She could see their flashlight on in the shed. She ran for it, only to get there just in time to see Papá emerge now holding his bat and a tire iron.

"Marta, get back inside right now!" Papá said, barking the order at her. He went back to the breaker box and flipped the switches to power up the house a second time.

"The thing is still here, Marta. The monster you and I saw. I swear it's here, I can feel it," Mateo whispered so their father would not hear. He was still clutching the kitchen knife.

"We need to get inside. Mamá can call Tía Lupe. She'll know what to do," Marta answered.

Her eyes darted to the back fence almost reflexively, half expecting to see yet another horror in the flesh. As soon as they were all back in the house again, Papá locked everything up tight and made everyone stay in the living room so they were all together. He had not witnessed the young girl on the roof when Marta told him about what she saw outside, but he did believe that someone was absolutely causing these disturbances now. The lights continued to flicker off and on while they huddled in the main room.

"Call Tía Lupe," Marta said, turning to her mother then. Mamá immediately looked over at Papá, who stared back at her, lost and confused.

"Call Lupe? For what?" he asked.

Papá had always maintained cool feelings toward Tía Lupe because he found her methods bizarre and he thought her prone to a kind of hysteria whenever he witnessed her healing prayer rituals in the past. Not that this had ever stood in the way of her relationship with Mamá. He always preferred to keep his opinions largely to himself, even though his feelings on Tía Lupe's ways were both obvious and known to everyone anyway, including Tía Lupe.

Mamá stared helplessly at her husband. Her eyes were silently pleading, unsure of even how or where to begin with the truth about what was happening now or over the last couple of days. Without answering him, she walked over to the phone to dial up her sister. Before he could ask another question, Marta stepped in front of him and began to explain. Mateo joined alongside her, prepared to back up every word and make their father understand. Just then, they heard Mamá let out a quiet gasp. Marta turned around to see their mother holding up the phone, a look on her face that Marta could not even describe.

"What is it?" Dahlia, who was standing closest to Mamá, asked.

"The phone line is dead," Mamá answered back.

They were on their own. Their night stretched on in agony, and no one left the living room. They sat there in darkness as the footsteps continued on the roof well into the wee hours of the morning. As much as Papá wanted to go back outside and address whoever was up there, Mateo and Marta had now told him everything, including what happened while Tía Lupe conducted *la limpia* over the house. He was not sure what to make of it all, but after a full night of experiencing this unrelenting harassment and terror for himself, he was beginning to accept that something far more powerful than any of them was behind this. He was truly afraid now, wondering how he was going to protect his family.

Marta stayed on the couch close to Dahlia, clutching her hands. While Mamá recited her prayers silently nearby, Marta thought about the girl on the roof.

"What did she mean when she said she had come for you?" Dahlia asked.

"I have no idea," Marta answered.

She thought back to the shadow she dreamt the night before that gripped her by the arm. That horrible creature, the monster, was still out there, as if standing guard in their yard. Marta shuddered, her body suddenly feeling very heavy, like it was sinking into the ground. She felt like she was marked now, somehow. The dreams had been a message, telling her something terrible was coming. She understood that now, and she quietly cursed herself that she had not put it together sooner, thinking maybe there was something she could have done then. Marta now sat there on the couch, petrified that something was already here and there was no way of stopping it. She also could not shake the feeling that there was something about the ghost of the young girl that felt familiar to her. It was almost as if Marta knew her somehow.

Mateo and Papá stood guard at the doors of the house all night while Mamá and Dahlia slept in fits and starts. Marta dared not close her eyes because she knew what waited for her if she did. Just before dawn broke through the night sky however, she nodded off. In her dream she could clearly see Mateo slumped in his chair by the back door, still clutching the flashlight as he slept, and right on the other side, hovering there, was the same hideous creature she had first seen. The beast. Standing with its head still tilted sickeningly to the side. She knew it had been waiting there all night. Marta knew it was there even in the daylight when she could not see it. And she knew that whatever had brought it to them had also brought the young woman. They were connected, and somehow so was Marta. She woke up to the sounds of her own crying.

Chapter 12

El Guardia de Las Tumbas. The guard of the graves. This was the wolf creature that was holding vigil in their yard night after night, the one that tormented Marta and Mateo. Tía Lupe explained to them all when they showed up on her doorstep the next morning looking disheveled and weary, all of them with dark circles under their eyes.

"*El Guardia de Las Tumbas* is a forsaken creature. He exists between heaven and hell, *mi corazon*. He stays trapped in purgatory and he must stand watch over the bodies of the dead for all time," Tía Lupe said, her hands busy heating fresh tortillas on the *comal* for her sister and the family. "You mean to say you've seen him? In the flesh??" she added.

Tía Lupe sat down with them while they ate the *caldo de pollo* she served when they first arrived. It was quite simply the best homemade chicken soup any of them could remember tasting in what felt like forever, and for what seemed like a few minutes, no one spoke. They could only savor every nourishing flavor and morsel as they ate.

"I have seen him in my dreams and when I am awake, and Mateo has seen him as well," Marta answered, shaking as she tried to process what her Tía was telling her.

This was almost unfathomable to Marta. She looked over at

Mateo and then at her father to try to gauge what they were thinking. Mateo focused solely on Tía Lupe, looking equally stunned by this revelation, and Papá kept his eyes on his soup. She could see that his hands were trembling as he broke pieces of tortilla and attempted to eat. She never saw her father show true fear and the sight of it on him now shook her much more than she would have anticipated.

"I can't say I know anything about the young woman you saw on the roof, Marta, but the creature you're describing, that's *El Guardia*," Tía Lupe said.

"I feel like they are connected, the woman and *El Guardia*," Marta replied, though she still did not understand how or why.

"It could be," Tía Lupe answered, "If this woman is a spirit, as you say, it may be that he's here because she's here."

And she is here because of me, Marta thought to herself again. Mamá seemed to have the same intuition just then because she quietly chimed in.

"We need protection over Marta. Protection over all of them," she said, motioning to Marta, Dahlia and Mateo.

Dahlia had not said much of anything since morning had come. She had been so unmoored once they had all woken up that she slowly paced about the house, her eyes focused on nothing, as they all readied themselves. Mamá watched her carefully and kept squeezing Dahlia's hand every time she slowly walked by. The thin lines of dirt had come back on the inside of every windowsill in the night and upon seeing the lines there in the morning, they all agreed that the best thing they could do now was pay Tía Lupe a visit.

Hearing Mamá's request for the kids, Tía Lupe turned now to face Papá.

"*Debes confiar en mí ahora,*" she said to him. *You must trust me now.*

It was not that he had grown up with any less of the same folk remedies that Mamá had. These traditions, this ancestral legacy, had been in his family too since well before Texas was ever Texas. Papá knew he would have to put his trust in his sister-in-law now because he had just been through a night of torment with his family that he could neither explain nor understand, and he had been powerless to protect any of them. He had never felt so defenseless in his life. He nodded at Tía Lupe both in humbled defeat and gratitude for anything she could do for them. She quietly nodded in return, a new alliance now formed between them. She then directed Marta, Dahlia, and Mateo to make their way to the small sitting room in the front of the house.

Tía Lupe had lived on a *ranchero* for all of Marta's life. She had sweet childhood memories of running around chasing her Tía's chickens and feeding the goats there. In Marta's early years, she remembered that the floors of the house were just packed dirt, but Papá and a neighbor laid floorboards for her throughout the house when Marta was in grade school. Fresh flowers always colored her home, for Tía Lupe was no less a fantastic gardener than Mamá was. So much so in fact that it nearly felt to Marta like a genetic trait that was passed down like any other. Except in Marta's case, she had needed to be a careful student, exact in her methods to produce even remotely similar results as her mother and Tía ever did. They were just naturals. Tía Lupe also maintained a vast collection of dried herbs and oils that she used in her rituals, along with drying racks in the kitchen that she hung herbs and plants from.

From the kitchen, she came to join them in the main room carrying some *chilchil de cerro, santa maria, pennyroyal, altamisa and laurel,* all plants she used for medicinal purposes. She brushed the fresh green bundle with a fragrant oil and swept the bouquet over Marta, her brother, and her sister in large brush strokes as she whispered the prayer for the Angel of God. The prayer's purpose was to cast out the dark forces that had invaded their minds and were made real before their eyes.

As she closed her eyes to take in her Tía's words, she felt an anger rise within her. This attack on her household had plagued her and so far, it had been getting the better of her. She could not surrender her mind and heart to it. Her mind traveled the distance back out to their home. She saw their front porch and the young girl standing at their doorstep staring back at her.

What do you want from me? The question formed in Marta's mind.

I can't leave without you. The girl answered back.

Marta opened her eyes and took a deep breath as Tía Lupe finished her recitations and did a final sweep of the herb bundle over the three of them. She handed their mother freshly prepared prayer candles and a jar full of some kind of herbal concoction with a variety of minerals. It was for Mamá to pour across the threshold to the doors of the house and on the outer sills of every window while she said the Rosary.

"Everywhere *El Guardia* could get in," Tía Lupe instructed. It was meant to ward off evil and harm.

Papa fidgeted on the couch as all of this unfolded. Split between wanting his family to receive whatever comfort and care Tía Lupe could provide and trying to devise a plan of his own for how he was going to protect them. A new night, and with it a new threat, was approaching. He ran through everyone he knew across town and tried to figure out if there was anyone that might take them in if necessary while they dealt with what was happening at home.

"You know you can always come here. No matter the hour," said Tía Lupe.

She seemed to have been looking at him and understood what was troubling Papá's mind. He gave her a weary smile and Mamá hugged her as they tearfully said their goodbyes. Without even discussing it with her parents, Marta knew why it would do no good to take Tía Lupe up on the offer for a sanctuary. The young woman had told her she couldn't leave without her and that meant none of this could come to an end so long as Marta tried to run. It had found her once already, in her own home. In her own bed. It could find her anywhere she went.

When they got back to their house, the late afternoon sunset was showing vibrant pinks, oranges, purples and blues as the whisper of a moon began to peak out and dusk settled in. Mamá had a note taped to her storefront's door. She pulled it down to inspect its contents. It was from one of the ladies somewhere in the community saying Mamá's store was missed today and hopefully she would be open for business tomorrow.

"*Ayúdame*," she said quietly to herself, and tucked the note in her pocket. *Help me.*

Marta wasn't sure who she was directing that plea to, but she noted the sorrow in her mother's face as she said it. They all slowly ascended the porch steps and entered the home, their bodies slowed with exhaustion as if they were wading underwater trying to push forward. This house, their home, held so many beautiful memories for all of them. How strange it was to feel as though it was no longer theirs. As though they could no longer claim a haven in it because a literal wolf had come to their door and with it, a ghost that haunted Marta's mind. There was nowhere that felt safe to them now. All they could do was hold on to one another and prepare to face the darkness together. Under any other circumstances, this unity might have given Marta some kind of comfort, but they had all experienced too much. She had felt and seen things too terrifying for her to rebound from easily, and now all she could feel was isolation and despair.

Chapter 13

He had been bored with all of this. When she came to him for help and told him why, he thought it trivial and a waste of their time, but the girl was adamant. He knew he ultimately had no say in the matter. It was written long ago. He would help her because that was his whole point after all, his purpose. He was a guard, just one of many the world over. In many languages, in many cultures. *Los guardias de las tumbas.* This was their sentence, their never ending purgatory, to serve the souls that lingered between the heavens and the earth. They also served the ones en route to the fires of hell. It was all the same in his eyes, and his eyes had been taking this in for centuries now. It was these souls stuck in the in-between who held the most concern over their ultimate resting place, if they were so blessed to even have one. Often, *El Guardia* was charged with keeping watch over souls who were never laid to rest to begin with, but merely left for dead. Left to linger forever where their lives had expired. He never told them that there was no way out for them, just as there was no way out for him. No one sufficiently prepared their bodies for the journey of the afterlife. Whether burial, by ritual blessing or some process wherein their bodies were given over whole to it, the living had not made these dead ready and this meant they would walk this path for all eternity, the in-between. *El Guardia* had developed a modicum of empathy for some of the dead in part because of this grim reality, but he had next to no sympathy for a lot of the living because of it as well.

The living too often exploited and distorted the wonder of life while they failed miserably in showing any deference to the rituals of death, dying, or even grief. How eager it seemed that the living were to navigate around death entirely to forget its presence, its steadfastness, as well as forget all those who crossed over to it. It reduced the dead ones to little more than a foggy memory in a living one's ever deteriorating mind. Indeed, their minds were much too simple to reconcile death with life or see the truth that not only could neither exist without the other, they were made so much more whole and complex by the other. To even try to erase death is to erase a core element of life. There were exceptions, of course, there always are, though only by a matter of degrees in his estimation. He took note of the living who did appropriately honor the dead and the practices of death. He saw these individuals as outliers of an old world. Even as their teachings tended to carry over to their offspring somewhat, he had seen over time how these practices faded more and more, like echoes that eventually disappear into nothing.

One tends to value their soul infinitely more once it becomes the only thing left to hold on to. The dead dominate the living in this respect. He had seen how fiercely the dead could guard their soul and unleash unspeakable horrors on any of the living who would dare to trouble it, however unwittingly. It was his to do their bidding and he could not deny that he had committed atrocities in the name of the dead's constant, and mostly fruitless, pursuit of salvation. The girl had never spoken to him before. She had been in his care for some six decades now and he watched at how she went out of her way to avoid him, not that this concerned him. It was neither required nor preferred that he endear himself to any of his flock. He needed only to attend to them when it became necessary or when they requested it. She had come to him one afternoon, afflicted with grief and near hysterics over what was to become of her.

"*Fueron ellos.* It was their doing. *¡Tienes que hacerlo bien!*" she cried. *You have to make it right!*

Once he was able to speak calm into the girl, they mulled over what could be done. What he knew, and did not tell her, was that he had foreseen this and had already begun preparations well before she had come to him. The living ones, one in particular, she had the ability to prophesy. It was strongest with her.

"Once this begins, it cannot be undone. We cannot reverse what we will have wrought, child," *El Guardia* said to her somberly.

He was eyeing her carefully now, picking over each of her grievances, scrutinizing them as if they were stones and he was inspecting their clarity. *El Guardia* knew well what she was asking of him, and he knew for certain that she had no idea. He also knew that she mourned something that was of no consequence to her circumstance, that she was one of the dead who would walk with him for all time, regardless. *El Guardia* did not say this to her either however.

"They must make restoration," she replied, anger pulsing through her like fire, "*No puedo descansar.*" *I cannot rest.*

"I will begin tonight then," he said.

"What will you do?" she asked, her hands trembling.

"Their minds are often the most vulnerable. The most pliable. That is where we begin." he answered.

* * *

She had been such a quiet girl in life. Always doing as she was told. She was quick to learn and did a great deal to help her mother out, caring for her younger siblings. So devoted was she in this manner in fact, that this ultimately proved her undoing. The family lost her baby brother to a blood sickness in 1901 and her younger sister to it just two years later. The girl herself finally succumbed to a yearlong battle with the disease the following year in 1904 when she was just fourteen years old. Her family had always lived modestly, but the years of illness and death had left them grief-stricken and saddled with poverty by the time she passed. They had rooted themselves in the community well though and it was plainly obvious to everyone that they could scarcely afford a burial, so Don Santiago arranged for the girl to be laid to rest in his little cemetery, *Las Flores.* People from around the little village came to the funeral and her family laid calla lilies with her. She wore the white Communion dress her mother made and kept altering for her throughout the years as she continued to grow. Her mother had selected the words for the headstone that the community had come together to make for her, including a special place for the girl's picture.

El Guardia was there the day of her funeral. He was standing with the girl, now one of the dead, towards the back of the cemetery, looking on at the living as they cried and held one another. He expected a cacophony of questions, confusion and anger from her since that was the rather aggravating custom of the newly dead, but the young girl just stood watching silently. Even in death, a quiet girl who did as she was told, quick to learn. For several years, her family came to the little cemetery every week, adorning her grave with a variety of special treasures because it brought them peace and because they were the things she loved in life. In time, however, it became necessary for them to move further north for work and the visits came less and less frequently. As the years passed, the living who came grew older and more frail. She watched her father's gradual use of a cane, her mother's hands become more and more changed by arthritis. She watched her one living sibling, an older brother, grow and bring a new wife to the cemetery. Then a new baby. Eventually, he became the first to stop coming. And one day, though the girl did not understand how or why, she knew her mother and father would not be returning ever again. Something had gone out, like the light of a candle perhaps. She did not ask *El Guardia* any questions about it. She just knew not to look for them anymore.

Years of solitude passed for her and she watched her grave and many others around her fall into various states of ruin. It mattered not at all to any of the others, but there was a part of her that longed for the days when she would turn to look upon her grave and see fresh flowers or a thoughtful trinket her mother might have brought to leave there. Even so, she worried little about this and mostly looked forward to when she might be received at the gates of a paradise beyond. She needed only to keep herself ready so that when that time came, she could cross over finally, as she believed it had been written. But then they came and brought desecration with them. It was this act of callous cruelty that twisted her then, beyond recognition. Anger engulfed her. It was fueled on only by a singular focus toward vengeance. Yes, restoration would need to be made, but this alone was not enough in her eyes. A price would need to be paid and it was then that she remembered that *El Guardia* was the shepherd they were to entrust with these matters. So she went to him and now she had begun a course of events that no one, not even *El Guardia* himself, could fully anticipate.

There was a time when she was among the living that all of this would have shocked her to her core. That her fire and fury would have so shamed her that it would have compelled her to go to her mother weeping for prayer and guidance to rid herself of such destructive inner workings of her mind. But that was then; she was among the dead now. There was nothing left for her to hold on to in any world and no world that wanted her. She had become altered and undone.

Chapter 14

One of the lessons Tía Lupe and Mamá learned early on in their lives was that there was nothing beyond the obvious aspect of the physical that was permanent about death. It was not the end of your spirit, nor was it the death of your love, anger, passion, goodness, or even your fear and malice. Tía had always believed that these things transcended to a different realm, but could easily move back and forth across worlds, both physical and not. Both waking and not. It was one of the reasons their family took such meticulously good care of the final resting place for so many other family members who had gone on before them. It felt too much like forsaking loved ones entirely to do anything less simply because their bodies had died.

So Marta understood that this young woman who had appeared and communicated only with her was as real in this waking world as any of them that breathed the air or housed a beating heart with blood coursing through their veins. *Your words won't help you now,* the shadow in her dream had said. She closed her eyes and she could see it approaching her as she lay in bed that night. She was not able to make out much of a face before, but now she could. Its black eyes were the same. That snarl, the low growl. It was *El Guardia.* He had arrived first, after all, warning her about what was coming. Warning her that no matter what they said or what mortal rituals they reached for, they could not drive him or the ghost of this young woman away. They were here to be reckoned with.

The late afternoon had moved by quickly. Papá had gone into a frenzy, pulling out tools from the shed that they could use in self-defense if necessary, including his ax. He also pulled spare lumber that he had saved up and began boarding up as many windows as he could with Mateo's assistance. Mamá and Marta blessed the jarred concoction Tía Lupe had sent them home with while Dahlia prepared it over the stove and let it simmer in water for one hour. After it cooled, Mamá went through the house, pouring it in a line just outside the threshold of every door and on the outside sill of every window. It had an unbelievably foul smell to it, but if it helped ward off evil or harm, it was a small price to pay for their safety.

The plan was to once again hold up in the living room, the largest of the house, so they could all be together if or when *El Guardia* or the girl made their presence known. Papá would be the first line of defense at the front door and Mateo, the first line at the back. Windows would be closed and locked and they would try to keep cool with the box fan from Mamá and Papá's room moved into the central space. If they could help it at all, absolutely no one was to go outside under any circumstances, since Tía Lupe's remedies could only fortify their dwelling. Every light in the house would be on, as well as the porch and flood lights.

The sun dipped down out of sight and the last of its light faded with it. It gave way to the early evening sky with its faint stars and that same glowing moon, luminous and large. A sweet breeze swept through the trees as the birds fluttered about in their final curtain call before heading home to nests tucked safely away. Marta looked out the window through a gap in her Papá's board work, taking it all in. It was almost peaceful. She longed for the sight of her parents out there on the front porch, conversing and cracking each other up while they enjoyed the beautiful summer evening together. To see Dahlia heading off to the movies with Yolanda dressed in her latest fashionable design that she had sewn together with Mamá. She longed to see Mateo's oversized frame trying to curl up on the couch while he caught *The Ed Sullivan Show* or lost himself in one of his latest books. Hell, she longed for the chance to do that herself. Blessed beyond riches they all had been, she realized, even despite having come from so little. Now she sat there wearily looking out their window for any signs of danger and mourning the normal world that no longer existed for any of them.

Dahlia begged Papá to let her turn the television on just to try to have some sort of distraction going while the night dragged on. They had been sitting around vigilant, on a knife's edge, for almost two hours and all was quiet for the most part. Paranoia had sunk in, so it was hard to tell the regular noises of an old country house settling in apart from anything far more sinister.

"I can't go on like this for the entire night Papá, let's just put it on real low just to have something to look at," Dahlia said, pleading.

He was far too preoccupied with guarding the house to really care what she did, so long as she stayed inside and did not make too much noise. Dahlia turned on the television and sat down on the couch. Mamá put her arm around her and held her for comfort as she inwardly recited another prayer. She had set Tía Lupe's homemade prayer candles up along the kitchen table, along with a few of her own things from her bedroom altar. Mamá felt confident that she followed every one of Tía's instructions to the letter and if they could just make it through this night without any more disturbances, hopefully it meant they had banished this darkness from their house for good. She expected to be exhausted when she opened up the shop tomorrow after being up all night, but she prayed it would be the last night like this that they would ever have to endure.

Nobody picked up on it at first except Marta. She heard what sounded like tapping on the window right above the kitchen stove. Even Mateo, who was closest to it, did not seem to take notice at first. Rapid taps that it took her only a few seconds to realize was the sound of something pelting their window pane. She looked out the front window through the slats to see if it had begun to rain but the ground was bone dry. Mateo was on his feet now, having heard the sounds as well. He gestured for Dahlia to turn the volume on the television down, and she immediately got up and did so. The pelting sounds were at both windows in the kitchen and now the window in Marta and Dahlia's room. Mateo looked out the window over the sink that looked out on the backyard and could clearly see what the pelting sounds were now. It was dirt. Loose dirt was hitting against the window, one handful after another and with increasing speed. The dirt was now being pelted at the two windows in the living room. Loudly and so forcefully that Marta wondered if the windows would hold. Papá only had so much wood to go around, and the panels simply were not enough to cover every window completely. Mamá cried out, grabbing Dahlia and Marta, pulling them away from the couch into the center of the living room.

"*¡Dejanos solos!* You bastard, leave us alone!" their father shouted now at the window, hoping that whoever was out there could hear.

Suddenly every window in the house rattled with such fierce pressure that everyone ducked low to the ground, expecting glass to shatter everywhere. Handfuls of dirt continued to pummel the glass panes in intervals, and then just as fast as it had started, it all stopped. For a few seconds, they could only hear silence and their own ragged breathing. A low growl erupted from the front porch and grew so loud that everyone covered their ears. Papá slowly grabbed his ax from the corner and took a step back, ready for whatever was on the other side to bust its way in. Instead, they heard it run off the porch and around the side of the house toward the back. Its footsteps sounded heavy and deliberate.

It's El Guardia, Marta thought. The sounds of the footsteps on the roof when the younger woman had first appeared to her had sounded nothing like this. These stomps were angry just as the dirt pelting their windows had sounded angry.

"Dahlia, call the police," Mamá said, whispering. Papá put his hand up to stop her.

"What do you think they're going to do? You think they'll help us? They'll just say we're crazy," he said.

It was absolutely true that *if* the police even made it out to their home at some point that night, they would not be particularly helpful. For starters, what was Marta's family even reporting? None of it was to be believed. If they did not dismiss the family outright for being hysterical, the officers would just tell them to continue holding up inside and to keep the doors locked for their protection. That would be it. *La policía* were never particularly keen on patrolling the poorer, browner communities of their town. The more rural the area, the less likely you were to get any kind of timely assistance. If they happened back by to check on the family at all, it would not be until morning and who knows what would have happened to them by then.

"We need to stay together," Papá said, meeting Mamá's eyes with a pained look.

She nodded in silent agreement. Just then a loud bang sounded on the back door as if someone or something was pounding on it from the outside and the force of it was so strong and unexpected, it caused everyone to scream. Papá crossed the room to stand with Mateo, his body charging ahead before his mind could catch up. He was furious now; he would be damned if anything was going to attack his family and his home anymore. As far as he was concerned, this was ending right now. Suddenly, the lights from all the prayer candles blew out and every light in the house shut off, leaving the five of them standing there trembling in the dark.

Chapter 15

Mamá scrambled to relight the candles on the table with the box of matches she had put in her pocket but before she could even strike the first match, the family watched in horror as something unseen yanked two of the candles out of thin air and flung them against the kitchen windows with such force that they shattered both panes.

"Come with me!" Papá called over his shoulder to Mateo, who had ducked low to avoid getting hit by one of them.

Breaking with his own initial plan, Papá unlocked the latches and threw open the door, all but flying down the porch steps with his ax positioned on his shoulder like a baseball bat, ready to swing. It took a matter of seconds for him to find it as he peered into the darkness of the backyard, straining to see under the moonlight. *El Guardia* was standing at the back fence, his face in a hideous glare, his long sharp teeth bared as he growled. If the sight of this monster rendered Papá petrified at all, it did not show. Without waiting for his son, he took off, racing full speed ahead towards the beast.

"No!" Mateo screamed, running down the stairs to catch up to his father as Dahlia and Mamá cried out after them both.

Marta was on her feet too now, grabbing the tire iron from Papá's stash of equipment-turned-weapons. She thought about doing what she had been told to do if this happened, because Papá had a contingency for this as well. If for any reason he and Mateo had to step outside the house, her job was to seal the house shut and protect the family. The very idea of leaving her father and brother to fend for themselves out there was inconceivable, but she knew he was counting on her and she could not leave Dahlia and Mamá on their own. She went over to the door and began closing it back up while Dahlia ran to the phone. She was going to try to call Yolanda at least and have her send help over. Yoli had no idea what was happening, but that didn't matter. Dahlia would figure out how to explain it to her later. Right now, they needed to get someone over to help Papá and Mateo.

"You can't Dahlia. The power is out," Mamá said, reminding her. Dahlia slammed the phone down as frustrated tears were forming in her eyes. There was no way to get word to anyone.

"Maybe I can run down the road and see if Ignacio is home?" Marta offered.

She began to reach for her tire iron again and a flashlight when they heard soft footsteps running across the roof. It was the girl. All at once, her steps were at the front door and a powerful wind blew through the house then, pushing the front door wide open. Dahlia and Mamá had never seen her before until now. They screamed and backed into the kitchen while Marta froze in her spot. The girl with no eyes looked right at her, right through her, and Marta could not look away. She moved across the threshold floating, like a shadow in the room.

Like the shadows of my nightmares, Marta thought.

Again, there was something about her that seemed almost familiar to Marta, as if she knew her somehow, though she could not imagine how or why. As the girl inched closer, Mamá held up her rosary and began reciting a prayer to cast darkness from her house, but the girl continued to move forward freely.

I can't leave without you. The words returned in Marta's frantic mind and she knew they belonged to the girl.

"Slip out the back door now, run to the truck and go bring back help," Marta said in a whisper to her mother and sister, her voice rasp.

"Marta, I'm not leaving you," Mamá answered, trying to keep her voice low.

Marta knew it would be futile to argue, so she turned to Dahlia then and they locked eyes. Dahlia was terrified to take a single step, but she knew this was their only chance and Marta was in danger. She grabbed the keys off the key hook and unlocked the back door as fast as she could, and then she was gone. *Buena suerte hermanita,* Marta thought, her eyes watering with tears. *Good luck, little sister.* She prayed Dahlia made it back sooner rather than later. Meanwhile, the young girl's face stayed on Marta's and she inched closer.

"*¡Quédate atrás!*" Mamá shouted as she put herself in between Marta and the young girl. "Get back!" she said again.

Before her mother could say or do anything else, Marta saw the girl reach her hand out, taking control of Mamá's body. She tossed Mamá violently into the hallway and it knocked her unconscious. Marta cried out and tried to run to her mother, but the girl reached her hand out again and pinned Marta to the wall so she could not move.

"Let me go!" Marta screamed, "Mamá! Mamá, answer me!"

Marta tried to twist and writhe her way free, but every time she did, the girl's hold on her clamped down even harder like a vice. She continued to drift across the living room until she stood right before Marta, her eye sockets huge and terrifying.

As the girl slowly extended her hand, she gripped Marta's arm, hard. It was so ice cold it felt like it was stinging her skin. Marta closed her eyes and let out a painful scream as loud as she could.

* * *

Dahlia was on foot, running and growing increasingly alarmed because something was terribly wrong. She had no idea where she was. From the moment she had stepped off the back porch, nothing looked like it should. The yard was not theirs anymore; it was simply an open field. The floodlights were gone, leaving her completely in the dark with only the moon offering the dimmest overhead light. She rounded the corner to the side of the house, heading up to the front, but she immediately saw that the truck was not there either. Neither was the road. Mama's shop was also gone and the neighbors' houses further down the road had disappeared, too. For what felt like too many precious seconds, she stood in the nothingness bewildered.

What the hell is this?? Where am I?

The only familiar thing was the house itself. Dahlia made her way over to the circuit breaker on the side of the house and flipped the lights back on so that at least the flood lights provided some kind of visibility. Still, there was no sign of anything at all around them for what seemed like forever. Her mind was racing and panic was giving way to full-blown hysteria as she started running through the endless field screaming, hoping that anything would turn up that looked familiar or that someone would hear her. She would have run in the direction of Yoli's house, but she could see for miles that there simply was no friend's house to be found. Dahlia turned to run back toward home, desperate to get back to Mamá and

Marta but the house had vanished from her sight too now. She was just out there by herself. Dahlia spun around and around again, sobbing, trying to get her sense of direction.

I'm asleep. This is a dream, it has to be! Wake up. Wake up.

Dahlia pinched her arms, but it was not enough to bring her out of this hell and she felt herself starting to hyperventilate. At that moment, she heard shouting far, far away in the distance. She could have sworn it sounded like Mateo. Dahlia could not see any flashlights or any other indicator that it might be him or some other actual person, but without thinking, desperate to find any kind of help, Dahlia took off running. She ran toward the shouting as fast as she could, in a field she did not recognize, screaming bloody murder into the dark of night.

* * *

Her name was Yesenia. That was the first thing Marta understood once the girl had her icy grip on her arm. The girl had been Yesenia when she was alive. Marta opened her eyes to see they were not in her home anymore. Somehow, they were at the family cemetery. Free to move now, she took a step forward and circled around herself, taking it all in. This was all real, or as real to her as any dream she had experienced. For a moment, she considered whether the whole night might actually have been a dream. She looked out toward the old *cedro* tree at the far corner of *Las Flores* and saw Yesenia standing there.

"What do you want?" Marta demanded, her voice shaking as she tried to reclaim control of it.

Yesenia said nothing but kept her face trained on Marta's and Marta felt a pull to walk over to her. Against every thought in her mind screaming at her to turn and run, Marta slowly made her way over to Yesenia underneath the tree. When she got there, she immediately saw what it was that made Yesenia seem so familiar to her. It was because Marta *had* seen her before. There, right around the side of the tree, almost out of view, was an old collapsed headstone with most of the engraving so badly eroded it was hardly legible anymore. When it had been standing, back when Marta was still a little girl, the headstone had been easier to read and Marta frequented it whenever they went to visit the cemetery. She knew it was one of the older tombstones there, dating back to the early 1900s. She remembered it because it was one of a handful of headstones that had a photo of the person buried.

Hija de Dios, canta con los ángeles, the headstone had read. *Child of God, sing with the angels.*

It had a case sealed by an old dirty glass door and in it, an old photo of a young girl dressed in a white Communion dress. It was Yesenia. Marta could clearly see it in her memories now. She remembered that there had been a small key inside the lock to open the glass door, presumably so that her family or loved ones could change out the photo or place other special tokens inside, though Marta could not remember ever seeing someone visit her headstone. The glass door had a small crack in it now and it did not look like the key was there anymore, but her photo was still inside.

Some time in the late 1950s, the old tombstone finally gave way to the years of ground settling and it upended on its side where it lay, around the old tree. It was easy to forget it was even there and Marta had, in fact, forgotten until now. As she stood there staring at Yesenia and what lay right beneath her where she hovered by the tree, every single thing that had happened to her family the last few days was all snapping into crystal sharp focus. It was as if she was seeing it all for the first time, and she understood what it all meant now. Because there before her, in the spot where the headstone had once stood, was what was missing, the reason Yesenia had come for Marta. The reason Yesenia could not leave without her. There in the ground were two gaping holes indicating someone had disturbed the soil. Someone had taken something that belonged here. Marta had dug up soil for Mamá because she believed it would be good for her garden. They did not see the fallen headstone around the tree. Marta did not know it at the time, but she had brought *El Guardia* and Yesenia to their door.

Chapter 16

Papá took off shouting, running as fast as he could. He was in no condition for such efforts. He fully expected the beast to charge toward him. Papá knew when he ran off after it that he was setting himself up for an ill-matched fight from which he would not emerge the winner. To his surprise however, the beast turned away. It dropped down to the form of a wolf and ran out past the fence into the open field headed for the *arroyo*. The grass was tall and unkempt past the backyard. Even though *El Guardia* disappeared out of Papá's view quickly, he pushed on, breath coming in heaving gasps, his lungs feeling like they might burst. He was determined to find the tormenting monster and rid his family of it. Mateo raced after his father, hoping to get out in front of him so he could protect him, but it was no use. Once he got on the other side of the backyard, he had lost them both in the tall grass.

"Papá!" he shouted, *"¡Dime algo!"*

Mateo stopped in his tracks, trying to listen for any movement.

"Say something to me!" he shouted.

The silence that came back was terrifying. Somehow, he had lost his sense of direction and he had no idea which way he was headed anymore. The clouds were moving over and around the moon, covering up stars, leaving him with no real way to get his bearings. In fact, now that he was really looking around using his pitiful flashlight's beam, the field looked nothing like it did during the day. It felt like he was out in the middle of nowhere with no recognizable marker for miles. *How far had he come?* Mateo imagined his father alone out there battling the beast for his life and he hollered out for Papá again, but heard nothing. Just as he was about to run off in what he hoped was the direction of the water to check if Papá had made it down there, Mateo heard a scream from somewhere in the distance behind him. He whipped his head around and listened with his whole body in the direction he heard it. It came again. Piercing screams in the night for *help*.

Mateo realized he was hearing his sister, but before he could bolt toward her sound, a dark shadow coming from his right side leapt out from the tall grass, running at full speed toward him. Mateo cried out as the shadow ran him down, knocking him flat to the ground. He smacked his head against the hard, rocky soil and lay there dazed for a few seconds. Then he heard it. The unmistakable low growl of *El Guardia*. Mateo was straining to see, but his vision was spotty. Still disoriented, he let out a painful moan and slowly rolled onto his back, trying to focus his eyes on anything around him. He looked up and saw *El Guardia* pull up to his full height, hovering over him, snarling. Then he crouched down over Mateo so close to his face that Mateo could feel the heat of the beast's growl on his skin. This would be the gruesome end, he knew it. Mateo thought of those teeth sinking into his skin and the blood pouring from the wounds. He was not ready for the agony of it. Images of his mother, his father and sisters, they all went flashing through his mind. He could not have moved then if he tried. The pain was coursing from his head through his body in vibrations.

"Leave them alone," Mateo managed to get out. He could barely speak. Everything went black after that.

* * *

Dahlia was running in the direction of what she thought was someone shouting, but the shouts had stopped cold now. Without that noise, she was not sure where to go, so she kept straight ahead, the grass scratching at her sides as she ran. She thought she spotted something bright and stopped then, trying to focus her eyes on it.

That's a light, she realized, and she sprinted toward it, shouting the entire way for help.

When she got to the discarded flashlight on the ground, she knelt down and picked it up. Her blood ran cold when she realized it was Mateo's.

"Mateo!" Dahlia screamed his name and her voice broke as she choked back the cries in her throat. She willed him to call out to her.

Everywhere was darkness and shadow all around her.

"Where are you?" she whispered to herself, as her mind ran frantic, wondering what *El Guardia* had done to her brother and their father.

Dahlia cast the flashlight all around her in a circle in the field, trying to see anything, any clue. That was when she saw it there, amidst the grass a few feet away. The smallest glimpse of it, but it was enough to catch her eye. In the sea of brown, brushy grass and dead weeds was a smattering of white, and she realized it was a shoe. It was Mateo's old sneaker. She plunged forward, the sobs inside her threatening to erupt, until she reached him laid out there on the ground. He was unresponsive.

"Mateo! Mateo, wake up. C'mon, c'mon *hermano*," she said, willing herself to find calm. She knelt down, checking him for visible signs of injury, and then she cradled his head in her hands. Dahlia was fighting so hard to keep her head together. She still had to find their father and any kind of help somehow.

"Wake up! Please wake up!" she cried now.

Mateo groaned and his face twisted in pain as he squinted his eyes open.

"Mateo-I'm here, it's okay, I'm here with you, wake up!"

Thank you God, she thought and she tried to assist him. It was clear her brother needed medical attention right away.

Mateo slowly rolled over to his side and tried to get his bearings. *What the hell happened?* He could not remember how he had ended up here and then a flash of memory hit. *El Guardia.* The beast had nearly killed him and left him there in the field. Holding onto his sister's arms for stability, he opened his eyes a little more and looked around, still dazed. His eyes finally settled on her face. Dahlia, his sister. She had found him. Tears collected in his eyes and they hugged each other tight in silence.

"Where's Papá?" she asked after a few seconds.

"I don't know. I hadn't found him yet when the damn thing came after me," he answered gruffly.

Mateo was slowly trying to get to his feet with Dahlia's help. His head was spinning. He did not feel safe to stand on his own, so he draped a heavy arm over his sister's shoulder and she planted her legs firmly into the ground to help him stay upright. He tried to clear his head to focus for a minute.

"Which direction did you come from?" he asked. Dahlia pointed the way, and he looked, though there was nothing to see but dark fields.

"So then we should keep going this way," he said, slowly turning to motion toward the opposite direction. "We have to keep looking for him."

"Mateo, you can't do that. You can barely move," Dahlia said, but Mateo was not hearing it.

"Let's walk slow. You help me, okay? I'll be alright here in a few minutes," he replied with zero confidence in that assertion. Dahlia did her best to balance his weight and hold up the flashlight to guide their path as they crept forward.

"Should I call out for Papá? I'm scared to make a noise," she whispered, suddenly aware that if the beast had attacked her brother once, it could easily come back for them and do it again.

"Let's just search quietly and listen for a bit. Maybe we'll hear him," Mateo answered.

They moved on slowly and silently for another ten or so feet before reaching the embankment that led down to the *arroyo*. It was finally something they recognized. The feeling of relief that washed over them both in that moment was so palpable that Dahlia had to blink back more tears. There was going to be no easy way to get Mateo down that embankment. It was tricky enough to navigate even during broad daylight without the highly likely existence of a concussion. Dahlia shined their beam down over the edge and tried to look for any signs of life, but the light was too dim from that distance. They would need to go down there. *She* would need to go down there, alone.

"Here. I'm going to sit you down right here and I'll head down there really fast and just see if he made it there at all," she said, once again faking her calm. She was fighting every natural urge she had to give into her panic and that bone chilling fear.

"The hell you are, Dahlia, you can't go down there by yourself!" Mateo hissed back. There was no way he was sending his sister down the embankment by herself with some creature from hell somewhere out there hunting them down.

"Mateo, you can't make it down there, and I can't safely get us both down there. We'll both fall if we try." she said.

Dahlia was firm on this and it was perhaps the first thing she had been firm on since the start of the night. He knew she was right. Mateo could see the fear in her eyes, but there was also no mistaking that it had to be this way. He nodded in defeat and she helped him to the ground.

"I'll be back as fast as I can. I doubt Papá went down there, anyway. He couldn't have hiked down there on his own, but I'll just see real quick," she said, trying to reassure her brother it was all going to be okay. She had absolutely no idea if it would be, but lying felt kinder to them both at that moment.

Dahlia straightened herself up then and, armed with the flashlight pointed out directly in front of her, she began making her way down. Time had slowly carved away the embankment naturally. The slope was steep and, by any measure, it was a decent hike to get down there to the water. When they had been young and whenever it had rained, leaving the ground nice and soft, the kids used whatever they could find for a makeshift sled and they would slide all the way down from the cliff to the water's edge. In all her years though, she had never tried to go down to the *arroyo* at night; that was something her brother and the boys in the nearby area would have done if they were out looking for mischief or the chance to cool off with a night swim. Dahlia was moving carefully and deliberately down the twists and turns in the naturally worn down paths to the water, mindful of stepping with care so she did not slip.

At last she made it down to the water's edge and let out a little sigh of relief. A new fear popped into her mind then. The *arroyo* was not without the occasional alligator. Dahlia whipped her flashlight all around her, her breath picking back up now. It was a new terrifying threat to be on the lookout for. All was quiet though, but then that was when she heard it. The faintest of sounds. Not an alligator, but something else. It was breathing. Labored breathing. Someone was down here. She risked disturbing the silence and called out for her father.

"Papá? Papá, are you here?" she timidly asked.

No response, just the labored ragged breaths. Dahlia slowly took a few steps, listening and straining to see everything captured within her light beam. After what felt like forever, the breaths came again, this time a little louder and she walked a little faster in their direction. Pushing her flashlight past a spattering of the tall grass, she let out a loud gasp as she discovered the source of the sounds she heard. There on the ground, struggling to breathe with his arm clutching himself, his forehead pressed into the dirt, was Papá.

Chapter 17

"*¡Marta, corazón mío, despierta!* Wake up!" Mamá cried.

She had come to and found herself on the floor in the hallway when she looked out into the living room and saw Marta face down on the floor. She rolled her over and checked for signs of life, relieved to hear Marta's breathing. Marta's eyes flickered open, and she sat up with a start, gasping, her eyes wide with fear. She looked wildly all around the little room.

"Are you alright?" Mamá asked.

She was by her side, trying to calm her daughter. Marta saw her now and her breathing was slowly returning to normal. Remembering what had happened, Marta looked around the room as if she half expected to see her family had returned. She had no idea how much time had passed. An hour? More?

"Are *you* okay, Mamá?" Marta asked.

She remembered now that Yesenia had thrown her mother against a wall before she got into Marta's head and she had the vision of the cemetery. She threw her with such force. That alone could have been enough to kill Mamá.

"I think so," her mother answered, rubbing the back of her head a little as she did so. "My body hurts, but nothing is broken."

"We need to find the others. Mamá, we need to get the others and go back out to the cemetery. That girl is buried there. We took something from her when we took the soil in the buckets. We have to take it back, *El Guardia* brought her here to get it back," Marta said, her words coming out faster than Mamá could keep up with.

Marta could see the confusion on her face, but there was no time to make her understand. They had to find the others and go that very night.

"Is Dahlia back yet?" Marta asked as she got to her feet, looking around again.

Mamá reflexively looked out the living room window as if she expected to see Dahlia coming up the walk. Instead, she saw the truck parked where it had been all night.

"Maybe she's here outside somewhere?" Mamá offered.

"Just get to the truck, Mamá. I'll grab the spare key from Papá's nightstand. Go now!" Marta said before marching into her parents' bedroom for the key.

Her mother made her way to the truck. Once outside, Marta did a full sweep around the house, calling out Dahlia's name, but her sister was nowhere to be found. *Did she go on foot? Maybe to Yoli's house?* The thought seemed plausible enough to Marta. It would make sense that she would go to people she knew and who were relatively close by. As Marta loaded up the buckets of dirt from the cemetery, she tried to devise a plan.

If Dahlia was with Yoli's family, and hopefully she was, then she may very well be the safest of them all right now. Mateo and Papá had not come back home yet. God knows what had happened to them. Marta and Mamá needed to get to them immediately. Marta started up the truck and backed it out of the small drive. Mamá was clutching her rosary, silently praying as tears streamed down her face. They came to the corner where the dirt road they lived on opened up to a small clearing that allowed them to turn onto the field behind their backyard fence. This road was even less established here than it was around the front of the house, but the occasional vehicle made use of it now and then. Marta drove forward slowly, the tops of grass and brush hitting the underbelly of the vehicle. She scanned the field to their right and noticed some old tire tracks, probably left by teenagers joyriding not too long ago. She maneuvered the truck onto the tracks and drove out into the field for a while before the brush got too thick to move through.

"Mamá, I need you to stay here –"

"*Mijita*, no! Don't go out there by yourself!" Mamá said. Her mother was wide eyed, frantically pleading with Marta now.

"I've got to go see if Mateo and Papá are out there, Mamá. I need you to stay here and keep the headlights on to help me see," Marta told her, trying to keep her voice calm.

"Please be careful, Marta," Mamá said, fresh tears in her eyes.

"Take this too," she said, opening up the glove box. She pulled out the flashlight and pocket knife her husband always kept there and handed it to her daughter, her hands shaking as she did so.

"I'll be back as fast as I can," Marta said. She hugged Mamá and got down from the truck.

Marta made her way out through the grass slowly at first, wary of what might be out there late at night, and she looked in all directions for any signs of someone, trying hard not to miss a thing. As she got out further into the field and the reach of the headlight beams began to fade, she turned on the flashlight and shined it all about desperately, shouting Mateo's name every few steps.

* * *

Mateo had heard Dahlia cry out and knew she had found Papá, though he had no idea in what condition.

"Are you with him?? Is he okay?!" he shouted down to her, but if she was answering, he could not hear it.

He was trying to find any path down to help her when he saw the lights turn onto the field. They were still very far away, but there was no mistaking them for anything other than vehicle lights. He put his hand out on a nearby tree, still very unsure of himself on his own feet, and strained to see a little better in the dark, but it was no use. The car was still too far. He wanted to call out to the lights, but fear gripped at his heart. And then he heard the sounds of struggle. Mateo flung his body around to see what was behind him a little too fast and he nearly passed out, but then he caught the sound again, coming just off to his left. He saw the bobbing of a flashlight. Dahlia. She had found a less aggressive way up the embankment and was trying to make her way up, supporting their father as he limped badly, fighting to breathe. Mateo rushed as fast as he could to Papá's side and tried to help them up the rest of the way. They got to the top, where they slowly lowered Papá to the ground and Mateo knelt down with him, holding his father's head just as Dahlia had held his a little while ago.

"Who's out there?" Dahlia asked, trying to catch her breath while looking at the headlights far out on the other side of the field they had been in for much of the night now.

"I don't know. They just showed up right before I heard you and Papá coming up. I think he's having a heart attack, Dahlia," Mateo said grimly as he stared at his father, trying to hold on to him, letting him know he was safe now.

Papá had not opened his eyes since they had laid him down, and he could not speak. The pain was searing now through his neck, his jaw, and down his left arm.

"We need to get him out of here," she replied as she looked back out at the lights and saw the movement of someone's flashlight just past the headlight beams.

"They're coming closer, look!" she cried. "Maybe it's Marta, maybe they're looking for us." Dahlia took a few steps out toward the lights and shined her flashlight back toward them in response.

"Hello??? We need help!" she shouted as loud as she could. She no longer cared if a demon beast was lurking out there at all.

* * *

Marta heard that. Someone was shouting out for help and she could see a dim light off in the distance ahead. A flashlight? *That has to be them*, she thought.

"Dahlia! Mateo! Is that you?!?" she screamed out.

"Oh my God, it's Marta!" Dahlia called back to Mateo and then shouted back out into the darkness, "MARTA! Marta, we've got Papá!"

Marta could hear her sister now and she broke out into a full sprint, running as fast as she could with sobs beginning in her throat.

"I'm coming!" she hollered. And then Marta and Dahlia collided into each other, both of them shaking as they hugged each other and cried.

"We have to get Papá to the hospital, Marta. He's in too much pain. He can barely breathe," Dahlia said as they hurried back to where he was still struggling on the ground.

"Mateo is in bad shape, too. I found him unconscious out here in the field. He can hardly walk," she added.

"I can walk," Mateo said, sounding almost embarrassed. He cursed his helplessness at a time when his family needed him most right now.

He grabbed Marta's arm tight as she knelt down next to him and she grabbed his back. The relief was all over their faces. No words needed to be said.

"Papá, it's me, it's Marta," she said, turning her eyes down to her father. Her voice was thick with emotion. "Can you hear me?"

He couldn't answer, but he opened his eyes then and looked back at her, his eyes glassy, his breath coming in sharp, short bursts that seemed to be taking something from him with each exhale. They were running out of time.

Chapter 18

"Papa keeps a tarp folded in the back of the truck," Marta said to Mateo and Dahlia, suddenly remembering it. "We can use it to try to carry him across the field."

She bolted back in the direction of the headlights as fast as her legs could take her. It felt like flying and she cleared the field in what felt like half the time it had taken her to get across it the first time. Just as she started to enter back into the headlight's beams, Mamá took sight of her and breathed a sigh of relief. But she had come back alone, and she was running. For a moment, Mamá thought maybe Marta was being chased, but then out of the far left corner, cutting through the thick grass, came *El Guardia* in his wolf form. He was going to cut Marta off before she made it to the truck. Mamá cried out to her daughter as she got closer, but Marta was still too far away to hear. Suddenly Marta saw the beast for herself and she stopped dead in her tracks. Armed with nothing but a flashlight and the small pocket knife, she felt ridiculously outmatched.

El Guardia pulled up to his full height, his black eyes staring right at her, his mouth baring those hideous, jagged teeth. Marta quickly thought of running back towards Dahlia and Mateo, but she did not dare make a move. *El Guardia* was like a rattlesnake. He would strike the moment she moved an inch.

Her fear was excruciatingly loud. He could hear it. For a moment, it drowned out all else and engulfed the full field, but it did not distract him. *El Guardia's* focus remained locked on her and at length, he finally spoke.

"You must deliver what was stolen," he began, "And know that I must exact a price."

"I will," Marta managed to get out. "We will. Please. We have to get my father some help."

El Guardia stared back at her, his face completely cold and so devoid of expression. Marta realized she was holding her breath, waiting for what he might do or say next.

"*¡Maldito seas, vete al infierno!*" Mamá suddenly shouted from behind him.

He turned around to see Mamá standing in front of the truck headlights, holding a wrench she had pulled from her husband's tool chest in the truck. *El Guardia's* mouth formed into a twisted, sadistic grin as he watched the old woman tremble there before him. He turned back to Marta so that he could look her in the eyes one more time.

Know that I must exact a price.

He echoed the words in her own mind, and she was powerless to stop him. Then he vanished right before them, just like the dirt on the windowsills. Just like Yesenia.

Marta ran back to Mateo and Dahlia, dragging the tarp with her. Her mother was trailing her by a considerable distance, but she was determined to get to her family there at the edge of the embankment. They were gently easing Papá onto the tarp when Mamá finally made it to them, and she wept as she put her hands on his chest.

"*Mi corazón, no me dejes,*" she cried, "Don't leave me!"

Marta watched her mother's body wracked by sobs and it was

more than she could bear.

"Let's go, Mamá. We have to get him to the truck," Marta said, delicately reminding her of what they needed to get done.

Together, Marta and Dahlia pulled their father as he lay on the tarp. He tried to lie as still as he could, every movement shot pain through his whole body. Mateo tried to help them, but it was no use. His head was still too violently dizzy, so Mamá assisted him as they all made their way back to the truck. They headed straight for the one local hospital in the area that served the community; Mamá with Papá, Dahlia keeping Mateo stabilized as best as she could in the back of the truck, and Marta behind the wheel. Her thoughts were racing. She needed to get her family to the hospital, and then she needed to get the soil back out to the cemetery. Yesenia had made it understood that this was what she and *El Guardia* had come for. They pulled the truck into the emergency room side of the hospital and together, they unloaded their father carefully from the truck. Dahlia ran inside and had two nurses bring out wheelchairs for Papá and Mateo, and then they all wheeled them inside.

"Stay with them. I have to go, okay?" Marta said, looking at Mamá.

"Marta, where are you going??" Mamá asked, demanding to know. Her voice broke as she said it.

"I have to get the soil back out to the graveyard, Mamá. This will all end if I return the soil to the grave," she answered.

"What are you talking about?" Dahlia asked. She looked from her sister to her mother, confused. "Return what soil?"

"I'll go, I'll come right back. Stay with them! I'll come right back!" Marta called over her shoulder as she headed for the truck.

"Go with her, Dahlia. Stay with your sister," Mamá said,

directing Dahlia.

"Are you sure? You're going to be okay?" Dahlia asked. She looked in the direction the hospital staff had taken her brother and father. They had both looked so painfully broken and Dahlia realized then that it was only the women who remained standing now.

"Go! Go now," Mamá replied, and Dahlia nodded quietly before taking off after Marta.

* * *

They were speeding down the highway now. It was pitch black outside, with a thin layer of fog blanketing the countryside. Marta had enough trouble finding the damn place even during the day. She was straining out the windshield, trying to look for the right turn now. Dahlia was trying to help too. They had all been so used to Papá always taking them out there.

"Right there," Dahlia said.

She motioned to the little cemetery as it came into view and Marta slowed down until the truck came to a stop right outside its gates. They both sat there for a few seconds looking around, half expecting to see *El Guardia* or Yesenia or who knows what else, but it was eerily quiet.

"Each of us grabs a flashlight and a bucket," Marta said, directing her sister as they got out of the truck.

Marta went around to the bed of the truck and handed the first bucket to Dahlia, then pulled the second one down for herself. It was a lot heavier than Dahlia thought it would be, but they had just dragged their father on a tarp across an open field, so she hardly cared. They made their way through the gates and Marta waved her flashlight over to the tree Yesenia had taken her to in her vision. It was strange for Marta to think of it that way, but she supposed that was what it was, a vision. They carried the buckets over and set them down in front of the tree. Marta scanned her flashlight around its trunk and sure enough, there was Yesenia's collapsed headstone on its side. Abandoned and forsaken.

"Is that hers?" Dahlia asked.

Marta had filled her in on the way, expecting a litany of questions and skepticism, but Dahlia stayed quiet, taking it all in, which Marta was grateful for.

"It is. And this is the space where we shoved the dirt into the buckets," Marta answered. She pointed the flashlight over to two spots in the ground where the soil had obviously been dug up.

"Let's dump the buckets out and then get out of here. We need to get back to Mamá," Marta said. They got to work spreading the soil out across the ground.

Under the beams of the flashlights as they worked, Marta emptied her bucket and began smoothing out the dumped soil when she felt her hands run over something jagged. She fished around until she found it. A small old key. She held it up and took a closer look, turning it over in her hand, a puzzled expression on her face.

"What's that?" Dahlia asked.

She had finished spreading out her bucket and was now looking at Marta, wondering why her sister had stopped. All at once, Marta knew exactly what it was and her blood turned cold. She remembered seeing it all those years ago as a child. Back then, it was always in the lock that it opened, waiting to be turned. It was the key that unlocked the case with the glass door to a photo of a girl in a white Communion gown. It belonged to Yesenia. They had taken Yesenia's key.

"Oh my God," Marta whispered.

She rushed over to the tombstone on the side of the tree. Marta ran her fingers over the crack in the case door and stared at Yesenia's photo. She looked so young. So young and so alone. Quickly, Marta inserted the key into the little lock and pressed her palm to the glass for just a moment, holding it there.

"Marta, we need to go," Dahlia said quietly now.

She didn't know what her sister was staring at over by the fallen down tombstone but Dahlia understood the two empty buckets meant they had done what they came here to do and she wanted to leave as quickly as possible. They loaded up in the truck, Marta turning to look back at the cemetery one more time, and they drove away back to the hospital.

* * *

When they arrived back at the emergency room, the triage nurse directed them back to another waiting room where they were told their mother would be. They made their way down the corridor and as soon as they pushed past the double doors into another corridor with a waiting room off to the side, they spotted her. Mamá was all by herself on the ground, weeping, her face buried in her trembling hands.

"Mamá, what is it?? What happened? How are they?" Marta asked as the girls ran over to help her up. Mamá said nothing in reply, and Marta felt the panic rise up in her belly.

"Is Papá alright?" she asked again, softer.

Mamá looked up at both of her girls then and they knew the answer. Their mother's entire body rocked violently. Tears and snot smeared her face. Every laugh line and wrinkle on her face distorted into something that was sheer agony. Their father was dead. Marta ran to the trash can over by a waiting room chair and threw up.

Chapter 19

Tía Lupe showed up the very next morning to set herself to work, maintaining the house and setting up for the visitors that were to come. Truth be told, she was the only one who possibly could at this point. Mamá moved about the house like a ghost herself. She was shell-shocked and beaten down by an unrelenting grief. Mateo had to bide much of his mourning alone in the girls' bedroom that they had freed up for him, recovering from the not insignificant concussion he sustained in the field the night before. Marta and Dahlia threw themselves into the funeral arrangements so as to relieve Mamá of that nightmare, though she made her one requirement plain straight away. They would not bury Papá in that little cemetery. As far as she was concerned, no one else from their family would ever be buried there.

"We just couldn't get him to the hospital in time," Dahlia said, as tears started rolling down her cheeks again. She brought her hands to her face. "If we'd made it there sooner, he could have pulled through."

They had just left the church where they'd met with the priest about their father's impending service and they were now both slumped in the seats of the pickup truck. Papá's truck. It even smelled like him. The last thirty-six hours had been a blur. The girls were running on practically no sleep, very little food, and it was all catching up with them. Any time Marta stood up or moved, the dizziness hit her so hard she felt like she might black out. They settled on the casket, flowers, the service, the plot they would bury him in over at Our Lady of Nazaré Cemetery, the newer cemetery further inside of town. They were both so depleted of anything resembling energy or strength now that all Marta could feel was hollow. It was as if she could feel herself disappearing and, for a moment, she wished she would. She hoped she would disappear enough that the wind just blew whatever was left of her away, like ashes.

"We can't do this to ourselves, Dali." Marta started, and she was going to say more, but she could not think of what else there was at this point.

The reality was that she thought it was the most sensible thing in the world for her to hold herself responsible forever for the death of her father. She was the one who took Yesenia's key, after all. If she had done nothing, if she had told Mamá she did not think it was a good idea to dig up soil from a cemetery and take it home, none of this would have happened. *El Guardia* would not have come to their door bringing the ghost of this dead girl with him. He would not have stood in front of Marta in a dark field and told her he would exact his price. She did not fully understand what he meant at the time. She did now.

They drove home in silence. Marta's eyes locked on the road and Dahlia's staring out the window at the rows upon rows of cotton buds in the fields. They were nearly ready to be harvested.

* * *

First to come was the wake. Tía Lupe kept food cooking on the stove at what seemed like all hours of the day and night during the two-day wake held inside the little home. They covered all the mirrors in the house up as part of what Mamá called the *Luto*. It was a mourning period that would last at least until the burial, though Tía Lupe told Marta that when she and Mamá were kids, the *Luto* could continue for a year or more, really until the bereaved were ready to move forward. Papá's open casket was brought into the living room for family, friends, and those in the community to come and pay respects. All alongside his casket and along the floor right beneath it were prayer candles that lit up the little room as if it were a tiny cathedral. People from nearby as well as distant family brought food and flowers, which they laid near him on the floor. He wore his best suit. It was a navy blue one that he had worn to his cousin's wedding, and inside his casket Mamá had placed their family bible, a photo of the family together, and the wedding lasso they had been married with.

The evening was oddly peaceful. It was good to see the larger family under one roof for a brief time, and it seemed to pull Mamá out of herself a bit. She was talking with loved ones and visiting with neighbors. Going through the motions. Mateo, too, was trying to be on his feet again and be there for his family. He had spoken very little to Marta since the night in the hospital when their father died. Mateo had been in a separate unit of the hospital for his concussion, so when his sisters came to him and broke the news, he refused to believe it. He even insisted that they let him get up and go to Papá himself. Eventually, reality set in though and once it did, he was inconsolable. He cried himself to sleep.

The last night of the wake, the casket was taken away to be

made ready for the Mass and burial the following morning. Mateo was back in the girls' room while Marta and Dahlia were sleeping in Mamá and Papá's bedroom on the floor. Or rather, Dahlia was asleep. Marta lay on the floor staring up at the ceiling as she listened to Tía Lupe and Mamá quietly talking in the now deserted living room.

"It's gone, *mi corazón. El Guardia,* and whatever terrible thing was trapped here with him, they're gone now. I can feel this house the way it was before—" Tía Lupe began, but she did not finish. She simply placed her hand on Mamá's knee, attempting to console her sister as silent tears rolled down her cheeks.

"I know. I can too," Mama answered. "I just wish he was here to see it."

Marta laid there in the bedroom, her mind once again going over the multitude of failures she had committed that led them all to where they were now. The house was free of Yesenia and *El Guardia,* yes. It was true. She could feel it as well. But it was she who had brought that horror down on her family, and the price had been too much to bear. She closed her eyes to the sounds of her mother crying and, without intending to, she fell into the deepest sleep she had in days. When she opened her eyes some time in the early morning hours the next day, just as light was coming in through the windows, she realized she had made it through the night without a night terror or any other disturbance in the house. It had been as peaceful a night as any they had had before that fateful work day in the cemetery. It really was over. She stared up at the ceiling again and then turned her head to the wall on the right side of the room, where she immediately locked onto a photo of her father in front of his pickup truck the day he brought it home. He was laughing at the camera, his eyes so happy, the way they used to get whenever Marta would make him laugh. He was smiling right at her.

* * *

The morning Mass was filled with many of the same family members, friends, and people from the community that had been circling around Marta and her family for days. There was, of course, more prayer and blessings upon Papá for a safe journey and upon the family for their comfort and healing. Mamá wore a black mourning dress with a black veil over her head. Dahlia wore one of her best homemade dresses. A black A-line with shoes to match. Marta wore a dress from Mamá's closet and Mateo wore his one and only suit; one Papá bought him when he graduated from high school.

"We're so proud of you, *mijo*. I know one day you'll be a working man, you'll do great things," Papá had said. The memory played in Mateo's mind over and over like a tape caught in a loop that morning as he got dressed.

Once the service concluded, people made their way to their cars for the trip to Our Lady of Nazaré, where the funeral would conclude with the burial. Mateo drove Mamá and Tía Lupe in Tía Lupe's car, and Marta drove Dahlia in the pickup truck.

"Tía Lupe says *El Guardia* and Yesenia are gone from our house," Marta began.

"Yeah," Dahlia answered, keeping her eyes looking out the window.

"I feel it too. We won't need to worry about them coming back," Marta said.

"There's no reason left for them to," Dahlia replied, and Marta did not mistake the bitterness in her sister's voice. She paused as if she was reflecting for a moment and then added, "I don't really want to think about it now. Or ever, Marta. I don't want to talk about *El Guardia* or the girl. I want to just—" but Dahlia didn't finish.

She just shook her head and looked back out the window.

Chapter 20

"Do you feel at peace?" he asked her.

She was sitting on the ground, her hands in her lap, looking smaller and younger than before. Looking like a heartbroken child.

"No," Yesenia said, her voice barely a whisper.

"No," *El Guardia* echoed, already well aware that this was the case.

She pulled herself up from the ground and joined him at the back fence of the cemetery, where they looked out over *Las Flores* together. She had obtained what she needed from the girl. The family made right what they had done. *El Guardia* had fulfilled his obligation to her. All of it had been as she wished it. Now all she had to do was bear witness to that which she wrought, as he told her she would have to do.

"Did you not intend for this? Was this not what you demanded?" he asked, again already knowing the answer.

Yesenia did not respond. She just looked out across the cemetery and beyond it. Down the fields with rows of corn and further still. Her eyes looked and looked until at last she could see the girl from where she stood at the back fence. The girl was driving out to the cemetery where they would bury the old man. Her father.

El Guardia and Yesenia had watched the family the night the girl brought the soil and the key back. There in *Las Flores*, Yesenia looked on with her mind's eye, and with a kind of morbid fascination as the girls attempted to help their mother off the hospital waiting room floor. How low and doubled over the woman was in her grief. *El Guardia* did not linger long to watch. He had no feeling for these spectacles anymore, but Yesenia could not tear herself away from it. This magnificent display of emotion. Of pain. Yesenia tried to understand it that night, and for a moment she thought she might. Something in her registered the torment on their faces. It was as if she had seen it before, but she could not name it. It was on the tip of her tongue, but she could not remember.

"Why do they do this?" she asked *El Guardia* that night, as they stood out in the cemetery. The place they were both bound to forever.

"They are mourning," he said. "We took someone they cared for very much."

She puzzled over this revelation then. Had there been anyone from her time in the living world who may have also felt this loss? She could not remember. Yesenia looked back at the girl and her family. This family she had ordered the irrevocable ruin of. The more she watched them, the more aware she became of their pain and sadness, and the more she began to pull it over herself as her own. As if it were a new garment that she might cloak herself in forever. By her own design, Yesenia had ripped from herself the last part of her that resembled any of who she had once been. She had hollowed herself out with her own wrath.

"It doesn't matter, does it?" she asked, and the sad realization of it was finally coming to her.

"They restored what was stolen, but it won't save me in the end... will it?" she asked.

"No," he answered, quietly.

"Why can I never leave?" Yesenia asked. "Why am I trapped here for always?"

He looked out across the field toward the broken family and motioned toward them.

"Very simply, child, it is because you were never released," he said. "You were cared for in the living world. The evidence tells us it was so. The living ones prepared you for death, as they should have. They prepared you for your journey, but you were never released to it."

Yesenia searched herself for the living ones *El Guardia* spoke of and, after some time, she found them. There they were, she could see them clearly now. The day she was buried. A mother and father who wept openly for their daughter, for all the loss and pain that had afflicted their family. The way it broke them both. She could see them visit her tombstone year after year, watching them age, watching them until they were gone. Until there was no one but her, alone in a cemetery she could never leave. Yesenia found herself simultaneously relieved and devastated.

She peered up at him, searching *El Guardia's* face for anything resembling an understanding or kinship of some kind. Instead, he only turned and looked at her, unfeeling.

"You will remain tethered here. Like many others. There is no salvation, child. No world to come for us," he said.

El Guardia turned to walk away from her and then paused, "Yet even as I say this to you now, you will never stop seeking it."

She stood there at the back fence of *Las Flores* all alone. Watching for someone who was not there. Waiting for something that would never come.

Chapter 21

They pulled up to the gates of Our Lady of Nazaré Cemetery and a groundskeeper let the funeral procession of vehicles slowly make their way through. The morning had been merciful in that it had a lovely breeze that kept everyone feeling cool and thankfully the sun had gone into hiding behind clouds by the time Marta parked the truck right behind Mateo and Mamá, who had already stepped out of their car.

"How was she on the way over?" Marta asked Mateo as they lingered back while Dahlia escorted Mamá and Tía Lupe to their seats by the casket at the burial plot.

"Kind of the same. This is going to be the really hard part, Marta," he answered.

Because now came the burial and the finality that came with it. Now came the dreaded reality that the family would be on the other side of this loss. The side that meant leaving Papá behind, as they had known and loved him before, to begin a new way of loving him. It would be a new way that did not include him here. This was the part they all worried for Mamá most. It seemed like she had cried all the tears she had to give at this point and now, particularly with the black mourning veil shrouding her face, it was like watching a spirit move through the proceedings. She had somehow grown smaller and more frail in the days that had passed. A stark contrast to the woman who stood in front of her husband's pickup truck headlights and dared to challenge a beast from the underworld just days ago. Marta looked at her brother and nodded grimly, and together they walked up to the plot and joined their family as the rest of the procession parked and stepped out of their vehicles.

In your hands, Oh Lord,
We humbly entrust our brother.
In this life, you embraced him with your tender love;
Deliver him now from every evil
And bid him eternal rest.
The old order has passed away:
Welcome him into paradise,
Where there will be no sorrow, no weeping, no pain,
But fullness of peace and joy
With your Son and the Holy Spirit
Forever and ever
Amen.

This was the last prayer said for Papá by all who were there and then, somehow, it was time to say goodbye. Friends and family formed a line and went through, dropping a handful of dirt gently onto his casket as a means to symbolize that from the Earth we come and, in death, to the Earth we must return. Then, one by one, they walked over to share their parting condolences with Mamá one more time. Mamá graciously received everyone, even though Marta could tell just by looking at her in profile that Mamá was not doing anything with conscious thought behind it. She was not there. She was again just going through the motions, biding her time until she could be alone with her husband for one last moment to say all the things in her heart that needed saying.

When it was their turn, Mateo, Dahlia, and Marta walked up to their father's casket and placed handfuls of dirt on top. Marta felt the warmth of the soil pass through her fingers and thought of what it represented. *Ashes to ashes, dust to dust.* But Marta had taken that. She had carelessly and thoughtlessly taken what had once been carefully, heart-wrenchingly returned to the Earth from which it came. The cemetery was sacred ground, to be regarded with reverence, but she had disregarded that completely. Now she could only weep for the gaping wound it had left in all of them and the gentle, beloved man they were now putting into the ground.

Mamá was the very last to step beside the casket. She waited until most of the others had either left or hovered around their cars. Mateo escorted Tía Lupe back to the car and Dahlia and Marta waited just off to the side to give Mamá her privacy. She touched her forehead to the lid and whispered something only Papá would have ever understood. Dahlia cried on Marta's shoulder, and Marta held her sister as they looked on. After some time, when Mamá finished her goodbyes, she picked up a handful of dirt in her fist, kissed it, and placed it gently atop his casket. She walked up quietly to her daughters, and they wrapped her up in their hugs.

"Let's go home," she said, barely a whisper. As they made their way back to the car, Marta formed a thought she could not let go of.

"Dahlia, ride with Mateo and Mamá back to the house. There's something I need to do before I head home," she said when they reached Tía Lupe's car.

"What could you possibly have to do today?" Dahlia asked, bewildered to the point of irritation by the mere idea of it.

Mateo also looked over at Marta, slightly confused but less

accusing about it. Before Marta could try to come up with an answer, Mamá gently touched her arm.

"It's okay *mija*. Take the time you need," she said. Then, her voice lowered, "But don't stay long."

* * *

Marta drove her father's truck out and rounded the corner to turn onto the quiet highway where the rows of corn started. She was nearly there. *Las Flores* with its rickety gate stood quietly in anticipation. It was as if it had been waiting anxiously for her to return. Marta noted a strange feeling in her body pop up then that she did not expect. One of calm. Peace even. This place, which had been the nucleus for so much terror for both her and her family the past few days, somehow radiated beautiful serenity now. The kind of sanctuary that made her fall in love with it so much as a young girl. Somehow she knew in the marrow of her bones that there was nothing left to fear here anymore.

She stepped out of the truck and strode up to the gate, where she lovingly unlatched it and let herself in. The *cedros* swayed peacefully in the breeze, and the cicadas were belting out their love songs for all to hear. She walked by all the old tombstones, pausing at those of her ancestors, and then she reached Yesenia's fallen tombstone and the patches of soil they had returned late one night just days ago. The key was still there inside the glass door and Yesenia's photo still looked out at Marta, her youthful face watchful. Hopeful. Not yet betrayed by a life and a world that would eventually level her.

Marta knelt down and put the rose she had been carrying down by the tombstone. She touched the glass door with her fingertips and then she rose and ambled back to the gate.

So many emotions were swirling inside Marta as she took it all in. She had loved this space so much as a little girl. But too much pain had happened. Too much hurt that Mamá would never fully recover from. That Dahlia would never really want to revisit. That Mateo would always carry some level of shame over. That Marta would always feel responsible for. In that instant, new tears rolled down her face as the realization slowly came to her that her family would never return to *Las Flores* ever again. And neither could she.

When she got back to the truck, she turned and gazed out across the land one more time. She looked out at the little cemetery that had been as much a part of her family history as any living, breathing thing and somehow, though she would never be able to explain it to her family later, she felt all the souls looking back at her. Even *El Guardia*.

She climbed into her father's truck, cranked the engine, closed the door and drove home.

1971

The workers moved quickly with an efficiency that comes from years of moving through this kind of labor across countless acres. They bagged up grass clippings, weeds and overgrown shrubbery and loaded it all up onto the bed of the trucks, along with their equipment. The last of it was pretty much done. The cemetery stood looking dramatically fresh, a stark contrast to what it was just a few hours before when they had arrived.

For years, the Masons, owners of this little burial space, had never had to think twice about cemetery maintenance because of one particular family who came month after month and tended the grounds. But they had not been back in seven years now and the cemetery had become such an overgrown eyesore that the Masons finally relented and hired out cheaply for the yard detail.

The men had shown up in jeans, work boots, wide-brimmed hats and long sleeve shirts unbuttoned with light cotton shirts underneath. This was standard attire for long days of yard work in the hot Texas sun. As they wrapped up the job, they all started making their way to the trucks.

One of the workers, a young slender man with smooth brown skin touched by the sun and a shock of black hair under his hat, bent down to scoop up the last of the bags of clippings. As he did, he saw it sticking out just enough in the ground. He could have nearly missed it, a small key loose in the dirt. The worker picked it up, thinking it belonged to one of the other men in the crew. He inspected its tattered, dingy old state, the patina to it, and he realized there was no way it belonged to any of them. It was far older than that.

"*¿Qué tienes ahí?*" asked another worker. *What do you have there?*

It was an older man, who had been following up behind him.

"*Nada,*" the young man said and after the elder man walked on, he looked at the key in his palm again for closer inspection.

Just to be on the safe side, he thought, the young man quickly shoved the key in his back pocket, grabbed the bag of clippings and headed for the trucks.

Acknowledgments

First, it must be said that the family cemetery is absolutely real. I set out to bring to life the family ghost story that I had heard growing up as a child. I have obviously dramatized these events, but the trauma experienced in a little house in South Texas the night the dirt came home from the cemetery has been the stuff my mother and tías relayed to us children over and over throughout the years. The lights kept going on and off all night. The footsteps on the roof were terrifying because they never found evidence of anyone up there, yet the sound was unmistakable. My grandfather hollered out into the darkness to try to get whatever or whoever it was to go away. My mother and her sisters huddled on the little sofa all night. Nobody slept. To this day, no one knows what was the cause of all that, but the very next morning my grandmother had that dirt sent back to the cemetery and the disturbances never happened again.

I can't pretend it was ever my intention to write a book about this, but it was only after I started the writing and came up for air after a few days that I realized I had only written the first chapter. I knew I wanted to also include in this story some kind of depiction of what life was like growing up in Harlingen, Texas for my parents and our full family. That close-knit family that has always grounded us and continues to call us back whenever we need to remember who we are and where our center is. That place we all come from.

I also wanted to tell a story about grief and mourning - about what it means to honor the dead and continue to make space for the people we love in our lives, even as we must release them once they are gone. Portions of this story reflect my own traumas that followed the death of a beloved family member and grief continues to be a lens through which I create many things. I do not know when that will shift, or if it will. But I do know that I am prepared to sit with it for however long is required, and that there is a great peace in that as well.

That said, characters in this story are not meant to resemble any one particular person, though there are characteristics and certain elements written in loving tribute to family. Our core group that is Marta, Dahlia, Mateo, Mamá and Papá are merely the players through which we could explore this family tale along with the themes of pain and eventually, healing. They are not stand-ins for anyone in my life but I have come to love them dearly and I am grateful to have been able to write about them for a time.

To my parents: Thank you for being great resources in the capturing of these events and of life in the Rio Grande Valley in the 1960s. One could write a book just on that alone. You are now, and always will be, the richest storytellers by far.

Also, a thank you to my sister for being a sounding board and for being one of my first readers as well as a partner in fun, new endeavors.

To Alex: Thank you for being such a wonderful source of inspiration and for letting me get lost in the days and hours that I disappeared to write this story, which included kids' nap times and after their bedtimes.

And lastly, a thank you to Liam, Isaac and Noah. Thank you for always believing in me and for giving me such a world of joy worth believing in. All my love. Always.

About The Author

Valerie Gonzalez Street lives just outside of Austin, Texas with her husband, her children and her dog, Luna. She has committed herself to voting rights advocacy work for the past six years and enjoys painting and photography every chance she gets. *Soil Of The Gone* is the first story she has published.

Find her at vgonzalezstreet.com.

www.ingramcontent.com/pod-product-compliance
Lightning Source LLC
Chambersburg PA
CBHW020929160726
47993CB00005B/2195